Acclaim for

MARK O'DONNELL's

Let Nothing You Dismay

"Thoroughly hilarious." —*GQ*

"The author is a humorist and playwright who writes like Fran Lebowitz with a heart: his characters are as affecting as they are funny."
—*The Baltimore Sun*

"The worse things get, the more the hilarity builds—you start to want to catch your breath and bring Tad into your arms."
—*The Boston Phoenix*

"Wryly comic, sweetly aphoristic." —*Elle*

"The author's witticisms flow felicitously. . . . Mark O'Donnell emerges as a true gift."
—*Time*

MARK O'DONNELL

Let Nothing You Dismay

Mark O'Donnell is the author of *Getting Over Homer,* as well as two comic collections, *Elementary Education* and *Vertigo Park and Other Tall Tales.* His humor, cartoons, and poetry have appeared in *The New Yorker, Spy, Atlantic Monthly,* and *The New York Times Magazine,* and several of his plays have been produced off-Broadway.

Let Nothing You Dismay

MARK O'DONNELL

Let Nothing You Dismay

VINTAGE CONTEMPORARIES
Vintage Books
A Division of Random House, Inc.
New York

FIRST VINTAGE CONTEMPORARIES EDITION, DECEMBER 1999

The Library of Congress has cataloged the Knopf edition as follows:
O'Donnell, Mark.
Let nothing you dismay / by Mark O'Donnell. — 1st ed.
p.   cm.
ISBN 0-375-40103-2
I. Title.
PS3565.D594L48   1998
813'.54—dc21   98-15883
CIP

Vintage ISBN: 0-375-70096-X

Author photograph © Nancy Crampton

www.vintagebooks.com

Printed in the United States of America
10 9 8 7 6 5 4 3 2 1

to Fran, Denny, Tony,

Kathy, Maggie, Bill,

Chris, Maureen, and Stephen—

my sisters and brothers,

biologically and beyond

Then turn not pale, beloved snail, but come and join the dance.

Will you, won't you, will you, won't you, will you join the dance?

—"The Mock Turtle's Song,"
Alice's Adventures in Wonderland

To do is to be—Plato

To be is to do—Aristotle

Do be do be do—Frank Sinatra

—old joke

CONTENTS

Let Nothing You Dismay

1. Battle for the Earth

At first, Tad was relieved to wake up. Instead of his usual wish-fulfillment dream—doing weightless triple back flips and flying through the air for his visibly impressed, if nonetheless faceless, peers—he had been trapped in a nightmare in which beautiful, naked, and, worst of all, tall young men and women were menacing him with knives. He had been brooding late the previous night about his freshman week at Hale, where he'd been teased about his shortness and townie accent, even though Hale students are supposed to be liberal. Blending that nostalgic anxiety into the triple-strength brew of his own sudden unemployment, personal scandal, and possible homelessness, it was no surprise he then had the dream he did. Unfortunately, he had to escape from his imaginary tormentors into reality.

The dream had had a calm-enough beginning, and seemed to take place at a weirdly contoured college campus that was evidently on another planet, because although the black sky coruscated with garlands of winking stars, Tad knew it was this world's midday. Some of the dream campus's buildings were ancient eroded stone hemispheres, like Druid igloos or the eggshell villages he'd built as a child to rule over in the sand-box. Others were futuristic, seemingly uninhabitable crystals with flaring acute gables made of mirrors. Tad, a tourist in his own subconscious, had to wonder if this was a college or an amusement park.

He ventured into one of the jagged glass chalets and found its vaulted interior was full of exotic birds in flight, which even in his deep sleep he knew to be a glamorous but bad idea. True to dreams' subservience to thought, some of the birds immediately crashed into the mirrored walls and fell dead at his feet.

Perhaps because he was afraid he'd be blamed, the sleeping Tad then bolted, and began to run from building to building, desperate to find his dormitory, or at least the classroom he belonged in. After a tangle of moments, he'd found his alien dorm room, and then suddenly he was inside what was clearly the Victorian splendor of Hale's secretive Serpent Club, which in true (or, anyway, waking) life he had visited only once, late at night, with his drunk roommate, who was a member. The difference on this planet was that the club was lit by Polynesian torches (Tad worried for the tapestries), and the beautiful, naked, and, worst of all, tall young men and women—apparently they were college students and not amusement park patrons after all—surrounded him with the aforementioned knives.

In his dream logic, Tad had thought all this was a bit extreme even for a fraternity initiation. Then it occurred to him that this was a curvaceous but pagan alternate world, one where, like his own, he didn't measure up to its savage yet exacting standards. Here, though, their way of rejecting him was ritual sacrifice.

So, when the trapdoor of consciousness dropped him back into his own calm and assassin-free apartment, Tad had a moment of happy stillness before he remembered his sharp-toothed waking problems, and felt anxiety swarm back into his corporeal chapel. As he accepted the fact that he was awake, he recognized the nearby door and window as old friends and bedside guardians, first blissfully thinking he was in his childhood room in threadbare but safe Waterville, and then realizing he was in the flimsy sublet Manhattan apartment from which he was soon to be ejected.

He winced, shut his eyes again, and waited for the routine but excruciating sounds of construction that usually woke him. At an unseen site a few blocks away, every morning at eight, a sadistic symphony resumed, the world's largest inadvertent alarm clock. Tad didn't even know what was being built, or destroyed, but it always sounded like a gargantuan Darwinian battle between a groaning metallic pterodactyl and a solid-lead woodpecker about ten stories high.

A minute passed, though, and the silence still clung to the room, kindly, maternally. Where was its abusive masculine counterpoint, noise? The battery-powered clock on the wall made *uh-uh-uh* sounds as the seconds passed, tiny heaves like an ant doing push-ups. Then Tad remembered it was Sunday—Sunday, the day of cease-fire, the break between rounds of the fight, the day courtrooms are closed, bad news comes wrapped in color funnies, nothing can be repaired, and even God isn't working.

He lay inert, eyes still shut, still half-asleep, his human chassis on cinder blocks of exhaustion. As the inarguable atoms of daily life rushed around his head, he reckoned the date, as a sailor might calculate his longitude after surviving a squall. It was . . . December twentieth, or, as he and his brothers used to reckon it in their childhood eagerness to get to the big day, Christmas Eve Eve Eve Eve Eve. The holly-decked juggernaut was entering the home stretch. The winter solstice meant the next few days would be the darkest of the year. And, to compound the call to significance, it was also, as he'd realized, Sunday, itself a scale-model weekly version of Christmas—a stern miniholiday pressuring you to relax and be grateful, to enjoy yourself solemnly, and, above all, to belong.

The initial safety of the bedroom shifted into hard focus as Tad cautiously reopened his eyes. Every morning has its own birth trauma. Every day has its dog. The third dimension, even at its nicest, has dangerously definite lines and angles—the slash where ceiling meets wall, the furniture that clearly exists as obstacles (a mere twister could turn any chair into a deadly threat), the cookie-cutter assault on the eyes where violently rectangular windows leap into view, light blasting its dispassionate scrutiny through them from the crowded, windy, and heavily trafficked outdoors.

Tad could feel the drone and dross of the moving air, hushed but varying like indifferent applause. He sensed descending like silt the tension of imminent phone calls, the ineluctability of bills, and the mundane lurches and gurgles of activities in other apartments. He heard someone's footsteps hurrying toward him down the hall, which might have alarmed him, but he knew from experience it was a trick of the old building's ceilings, and the person was upstairs, not in this apartment. Outside, a drowsing dog barked, its own tiny territory invaded by its own nonexistent dogcatcher. Then a car backfired, and after the barking, it, too, sounded like senseless, snappish aggression. Elsewhere on earth, grass, plankton, arsenals, and populations grew. All this palpability presented itself to Tad as an opponent to be wrangled. Dreams you ride, but life you're supposed to drive, and it's a faulty, strictly manual transmission. He closed his eyes again. As a child, he had done it to make himself invisible to others. As an adult, he did it to make the world invisible to him.

He loved life's details, relished even its absurdities, delighted in the oddity of human and animal culture, but simultaneously dreaded living. He loved people when he was alone but was terrified by the dynamics of actual company. He was his own best friend and his own worst enemy, which averaged out to mean he was barely acquainted with himself. He wasn't anything so binary as manic-depressive, but both at once, and through his veins coursed a red-blooded blender drink of joy, fear, and confusion. He knew the celestial setup of heaven—angels, archangels, principalities, powers, virtues, dominions, thrones, cherubim, and seraphim—but whenever his father, the almost-superfluous press rep for the not very pressworthy mayor of Waterville (the town that was host to hearty Hale) mentioned offices like *comptroller* or *council speaker,* Tad closed his ears. He knew how plenary indulgences worked in purgatory, and how to pay Charon to cross the River Styx, but he didn't know escrow from escarole, and when people discussed hedge funds, commodities, or the Federal Reserve, he chose not to understand. He loved the idea of protecting the innocent and romancing Rapunzel, but in those arenas he was mainly a Soldier of Fiction. Even as a teen at Waterville Latin, his would-be wiseacre friends had adapted a flip slang greeting to feature him specifically. They'd usually mock-hail one another with "How are you? Mad? Sad? Glad? In between?" But as Tad's trademark edgy ambivalence became familiar to them, they adapted their greeting to "How are you? Mad? Sad? Glad? Or . . . *Tad?*"

He had been reading in his folklore studies about an ancient Arabian tribe for whom to touch a maiden was a commitment to marry her—a stricter version of the "You break it, you've bought it" policy—and at this moment he was similarly reluctant to commit himself to reality by touching his feet to the floor. He reviewed in his mind what the day ahead might contain, as if to find a carrot worth moving his ass for. Though he imagined himself isolated in life's melee, a small skewed-orbit Pluto in the solar system of society, he had still, somehow, been invited to seven different Christmas parties that day. They were all crowded together at a week's remove from the holiday's ground zero, because those who throw Christmas parties know that to do so any closer to the actual holiday would mean their invitees might stiff them to be with their more genuine friends and family.

Tad added up the invitations in his mind, and even as he tried to enjoy the pleasant fact—or fancy—that they were a supposedly lucky seven in number, it also reminded him that two competing theses were being written on the number *seven* in his graduate department alone, and he had better get cracking on his *Social Hierarchies of Imaginary Places* before someone else stole his footnoted thunder. He didn't really want to write it—the research he had yet to do was vast—but without it as a goal, his life seemed meaningless.

He breathed deeply and reminded himself that he had to look for a new job and an apartment, and the parties he was invited to, however unappealing several of them were, might yield some leads. Network and survive. A midwinter day's work. Besides, the most unlovable assembly may offer free food. He groaned (his last official act as a sleeper), swung his body outward like the plank pirates' victims must walk, and touched his feet to the floor. From air lock to space walk. Perhaps by Arabian standards, he was now married to reality, but it was in name only.

He sat up, thereby achieving full three-dimensionality. The sheets of his bed lay tangled and creased like those on a sickbed, or one where love has been recently made, but to Tad they resembled a relief map of the Arctic. He ambled listlessly to the bathroom, where he sat on the toilet and offered the gods of regularity a sacrifice he had made himself.

How could anyone ever love me, he thought, in his depression, when I emit shit on a daily basis? After a moment, he upbraided himself for upbraiding himself. Everyone shits, he reminded himself, in the same way he had to remind the very youngest potty-conscious students at the Excelsior School, where he'd worked until Friday. And some of them are loved. Of course, he mentally argued the case with his several selves, even the most loved keep the process as secret as possible.

Unsettlingly, perhaps because of all his recent trauma, instead of the single brown Germanic blimp that indicates solid health, there in the bowl bobbed a tattered yellow flotilla, feather-edged and legion. As the fragile archipelago swirled away in the flush, Tad was surprised to be reminded of the teeming circles of angels surrounding the Light he'd been admiring in Gustave Doré's drawings of Dante's Paradiso. The Milky Way galaxy itself, he mused, also resembles a toilet in midflush. Was seeing angels in the toilet or toilets in the cosmos—firmament as excrement—a sign of madness, sadness, or gladness? As long as you find things interesting, he tried to reassure himself, you will survive.

As he washed his hands, disavowing his dump like Pontius Pilate, he reviewed a few of the day's options, options being a rare opportunity for him. His family was gathering for brunch, but after his oldest brother Les's recent suicide attempt, the mood would be strained. One of his downtown artsy friends had begged him to attend a charity matinee of his one-man show, but however worthy the charity, it was still a one-man show. His graduate department at the Alternative College was having an open house, but since he hadn't done any work on his thesis for over a year, he'd be on the defensive, and he didn't want even to pretend to listen to people discussing their thousand-page manuscript on the futility of language. He'd just been fired from teaching at the Excelsior School, so showing up at their party would be arguably psychotic. One of his best friends from Hale had invited him for dinner, but Tad's strong-willed ex-girlfriend might be there, and as beautiful as he remembered her to be, he didn't want to see someone he'd misused, however unconsciously. There was another, unearned invitation he couldn't remember at the moment, and, finally, Dean Parish, a man with whom he'd had a disastrous single dalliance, had sent him an engraved invitation to a very fancy late-night soirée, presumably as a gesture of reconciliation. In theory, Tad liked forgiveness, but the prospect of seeing thoughtless Dean, for whom he'd mistakenly left thoughtful Angelo, his lover of five years, made his shoulders ache. All these assemblies were supposed to be sources of comfort and company, but with his freshly kindled brush fire of crises, Tad wondered if he could socialize while in a secret state of panic. The past three days had almost unhinged him, and there was no spiritual screwdriver in sight.

First and fearmost, he'd been dismissed from his job at the tony East Side elementary school where he had been the staff storyteller while he worked on his dissertation. His dismissal wasn't just a mere downsizing, although he had felt miniaturized to about an inch tall as he'd dragged himself out the playground gate. The crisp new principal, Mr. Hyer—as he insisted even the adult teachers and employees address him—had reflexively fired Tad when a prescription-drugged divorced mother had imagined Tad was touching her son improperly.

The fact was, Justin loved piggyback rides, and no one but Tad was available to oblige him, since the boy's real and indifferent father was off supervising a Hong Kong bank's navigation of the consequences of reversion to the Mainland. Tad took pride in the child's trust, and the fact that Justin saw him as large and competent. The only completely relaxed relationships Tad had were with children, because they embodied pure hope. They managed to find life extremely interesting; they were its happy ending, only at the wrong end of the story, as if God had gotten His film reels mixed up. More wonderfully, children looked up to Tad, and they were free of sexual and career agendas. Even their selfishness he found bracingly straightforward. They were as innocent as animals being videotaped, unaware of society's judgmental camera. They had no plan but the moment, few concealed emotions, and no business trips beyond make-believe. And, the joy of childhood included the fact that, except for refrigerator art, there was no paperwork.

Justin had chattered to his mother endlessly and enthusiastically about how much he loved Tad. It was a phrase the unscary talking monster puppets on morning television encouraged children to utter, and there had been a recent craze for it among the students at Excelsior. One jaded eight-year-old had even taken to saying it constantly to adults he disliked, as a kind of secret insolence, to watch them coo back at him like duped pigeons, and only when it became clear he was spoofing—he had loudly avowed his love for the janitor and for a picture of George Washington—did Mr. Hyer ask the student body to start saying "I love you" more selectively.

Justin's mother withstood the lovefest, but when the boy accidentally referred to Tad as "Daddy," the overcaffeinated and underoccupied divorcée, in her own confused anger, chose Tad as a scapegoat for her husband's abandonment. She had heard Tad was gay, and like many people with minds resembling country clubs (they only allow notions they're already acquainted with), she assumed this meant he coveted children. Mr. Hyer made no attempt to argue with the woman, who was also a board member. To him, the customer was always right.

Remembering the accusation racked Tad anew, like a hangover made even more arduous when you remember what happened. The charge was false, unprovably false, and Tad and most of the staff knew it—even Mr. Hyer probably knew it— but the principal served the board, however skittish in their wealth, and in this particular pecking order, Tad was the sacrificial pawn. Old Mrs. Lord, the previous principal, wise and firm and pressure-resistant, would never have yielded. She was a child-rearer, not a fund-raiser, and valued programming over ratings. Besides, she had her own gay middle-aged son, a marriage counselor who, though never married himself, had written the best-seller *Men Are Convex, Women Are Concave.* Mrs. Lord had doted on Tad's doting on the children at Excelsior. But Mrs. Lord was dead, and the dead lose all veto powers.

Tad needed to unwrap a fresh bar of soap in order to shower, and he squirmed at its sharp edges, like rubbing a wooden box against himself, as he lathered up under the spigot's impersonal torrent. How could he face the call to

Fezziwiggly carelessness when he'd never felt so careworn in his life? Garth, the actor who held the lease on this apartment, had phoned on Saturday with the news that he was leaving his national tour to return to New York and that Tad would have to find a new place to live. Garth felt that playing the starving but surprisingly well-toned Second Peasant in the forcibly induced hit Dickensian musical reduction, *A Song of Two Cities,* did him no good in the hinterlands. He'd accepted the same meager role as a replacement in the Broadway cast. Being an extra in a national tour was the lowest, by Garth's figuring—at least once you've ascended from community theater to the professional stratum—and being an extra on Broadway was a step up from that. It would allow Garth to audition to replace actors in featured parts, or, better yet, for a chorus role in the original cast of a new bad show. Above that, of course, towered the upper reaches of leading roles and actual stardom, and, as theoretical as life in other galaxies but just as dazzling a distant possibility, roles in television and—though its all-powerful name, like Jehovah's, must not be spoken, at least not to fellow actors—movies. Stardom promised exemption from being billed "in alphabetical order" or "in order of appearance." It was the far-flung first link to his name above the title, a private suite above steerage, the immortal boy in the bubble, the rajah in his howdah, unfireable above his supporting cast, fame as rebirth, the salmon paradoxically spawning itself.

That was all fine for Garth, the safety net of a Broadway salary, *Les Confortables,* but now Tad would have no home from which to look for a job, and no job to pay for a home. His old parents, who were flying in from Boston, would find this excruciating news, since as a graduate student in folklore, he was virtually unemployable. It would pinball off their unwitting prejudice to remind them Tad was gay and so, by traditional standards, a failure. It would ruin Christmas, especially after Dad's heart attack and Les's suicide attempt, so Tad resolved not to tell them. Self-doubt usually assures itself it's actually thinking of others. The people he'd see at the day's looming festivities would probably gloat inwardly or pity him, depending on whether they felt below or above him, respectively, and he decided to play those particular summit meetings by ear.

Several times as he showered, Tad thought he heard the phone ring, bringing hope or sympathy, but he knew from experience it was actually Garth's plumbing, which made the water pounding the tub floor ring at the same treble as the phone would. It reminded him of his adolescent apprehension, when he always thought he heard parental footsteps approaching his room while he masturbated, when in fact what he heard was his own pounding heart. Still, his superstitious side couldn't resist turning off the water to listen for the phone, only to be ridiculed by his practical side for doing so when silence followed.

Finally, he stepped from the shower and rubbed a towel on his still-boyish red mop. Red hair, he had long bitterly noted, usually indicates best friend rather than main character, dummy rather than ventriloquist, Jimmy Olsen rather than Superman, farmhand rather than love god. He shivered as his bare feet met the cold tiles—another soft thing about dreams: no floors—and stood on tiptoe to see himself in the mirror above the sink. On top of everything else, or, rather, under everything else, why did he have to be so short? Mimi, the coolly inefficient Frenchwoman who had come in Mr. Hyer's entourage to serve as his assistant, seemed determined to mistake him for a child whenever he appeared at her desk to ask why she hadn't done something she'd assured him she would. "Yes, little buoy?" she'd say in her cushiony accent. "May I help you?"—obliging Tad to remind her he was a colleague before asking where his photocopies were. They were never ready, but she spoke with such circuitous condescension, it was somehow Tad's fault by the time she turned away to answer the phone. Sometimes you have to be kind to be cruel. Tad suspected she was using her foreignness as a cover, to allow her to mock him with impunity.

There in the mirror, like a reluctant twin peering over the fence, was that furious baby face, downy and disheveled like Donald Duck, the face old ladies still beamed at on the bus, the face that had gotten him cast as the Littlest Angel, even though—already an expert on fantasy at age ten—he'd protested to his teacher that the whole story made no sense, because angels were created as God's minions at the dawn of time, and little boys didn't die and "become" angels. She'd told him this was a *make-believe* heaven, rather than the *actual* one. Later, he was assigned Peter Pan (surprisingly, a gratifying power trip), Oliver Twist (more passive but still pivotal) and, at Hale, that master manipulator Puck. Tad had liked being supposed elfin as a child—it had given him a feeling of magical power—but as puberty demanded he enlist in its debauch, his smallness had become problematic and somehow another symbol of failure to progress. He wanted to dominate, and most men and women wanted to dominate or protect him.

He was thirty-four now, literally older than Christ, about to hit the decaying side of the biblical warranty of threescore and ten, and everything he'd tried, including growing up, had seemed to come to nothing. He really wasn't determined enough to be a professional actor, and anyway, he found auditions humiliating. His doctoral thesis was now years overdue. His uneventful years of living with tryingly virtuous Angelo were now fading in memory, and he wasn't proud of the way he'd taken advantage of the one person, however intellectually limited and tone-deaf, who'd loved him unconditionally.

The only project he'd successfully completed was getting into and graduating from Hale, revenge for his dead grandparents, who'd cleaned bathrooms and served meals to the insolent rich boys there. He'd also cured himself of his Waterville accent, by dutifully repeating out loud the standardized dialogue on afternoon soap operas: *"Whom . . . will . . .*

Maeve . . . plot . . . to . . . destroy . . . next?" As a life's work, though, these were, at best, preliminary.

He hung up the towel without bothering to refold it. There would be no need to shave for a few days. He had done that on Friday, the crucifixion day, before his meeting with Mr. Hyer, which he'd foolishly thought would involve a Christmas bonus. Still, a slight red stubble glinted on his soft chin, odd, like paprika on strawberry ice cream. " 'Not by the hair on my chinny chin chin,' " he recited. Even in nursery tales, the males have to stake their self-esteem on their virility. The pigs prevail in the story, but in real life the wolf would win. In real life, the cat gets the mouse. The hunter kills the rabbit. That was the consolation of folklore. Jack beats the giant, but Jack could never beat the insurance company.

Tad shivered as he recalled his nightmare, and then remembered in rattled dismay that he'd unpacked his suitcase in it—there'd been a dorm room sequence—and so he must have left all his clothes behind in dreamland, and they were now irretrievable. After a moment, the illogic of his imagined loss struck him. It was a joke and a relief, and he shook his head in typically mixed grim amusement as he dressed. As his mother would have pointed out, had she been able to bear hearing about nudes with knives, he hadn't really been stabbed and he hadn't actually lost any clothes. So, life should seem good. Zero in some cases is a positive number.

He put on clean blue jeans and a white button-down shirt—a noncommittal costume that was innocuous to a wide range of social situations, a sort of sartorial Esperanto—and ambled kitchenward, past Garth's framed old fifties movie posters that hung in the hall. One hysterically advertised a forgotten sci-fi epic, *Battle for the Earth,* with the overwrought motto "Incredible realism claws at your disbelieving mind!" He'd never heard of anyone in the cast, but presumably they'd all once hoped this now-sunken venture might give them a leg up in Hollywood's classic mud wrestle. The lurid poster art showed what looked like an overgrown slice of pizza with everything making off with an ill-advisedly underdressed female astronaut, and Tad could only assume that here was a creature who was trying to marry up. He felt a pleasant discomfort at the squirming woman's pomaceous, radiation suit–bound body, but he figured he was simply responding as ordered to the poster's hard-sell fantasy.

Next to that poster hung a companion piece, promoting a similar slice of delirium, this one called *Colossal Planet*. Its fevered artwork showed a clean-shaven man in a torn loincloth, wrestling with the enormous pythonlike coils of a Princess phone cord, as the menacing face of a kitten filled the horizon behind him, its eyes twin crescent moons. *Trapped, in a world he didn't choose!* Unlike the picture starring the unearthly pizza, this film featured someone Tad had heard of, and hated. Tad Vessel, who played the man made microscopic, had been a teen star of sixties beach movies—the second lead, who usually wants to give a concert to save the seminary—and Tad's mother, who was almost as superstitious as she was taught to be by her ghost-invoking Irish immigrant mother, had named him after the actor because the young nurses in the maternity ward had all been talking about him with reverence when her son was born. Tad had to live with his name's insipidness, like a tattoo of a koala applied in ineradicable maple syrup. No nickname he promoted for himself ever took, as if his birth certificate were destiny. When Vessel had announced publicly he was suffering from AIDS, Tad used the opportunity to come out to his mother, only to hear her say, "It's all because I named you after him!" Since her own mother had believed wholeheartedly in banshees and demons, for her to be merely secularly superstitious was a kind of advance. "I love you in spite of that," she'd added, and it was the effortful way she said *in spite of that* that he'd had to live with ever since.

The kitchen's old wooden cupboards creaked and clicked even when untouched, as if apathetic poltergeists were browsing for food but didn't have the will to do so vigorously. Tad didn't find anything that qualified as breakfast in them, or in the refrigerator, empty except for one last cellophane-wrapped, rubber band-bound hot dog, a dachshund in a strait-jacket. There was also the leftover fruit salad he'd bought to be virtuous and had yet to eat. He was too tired to chew, so he put the salad in vegetarian Garth's blender, then watched the chunks of fruit disappear into a churning pink vortex, like the limbs of a swimmer yanked under by a shark.

As he sipped the grainy juice that resulted, the TV news nattered on in the background like a garrulous neighbor, only instead of yard sales, it announced tribal warfare in Africa, genocide in Southeast Asia, and a pending sexual harassment suit involving a dog owner on behalf of her pet, claiming a neighbor's dog had made unwanted sexual advances to hers. Tad sighed, and was startled to hear his mother's resignation in his voice.

The phone rang, and he answered it. Let the games begin.

"Hi, Tad, it's Bonny." It was his brother Les's wife. She was trying to be cheerful, but he knew she was under great strain. "Your folks got here last night—ha ha, you can hear your Dad editorializing in the background! Whew! He thinks every room is a political convention! Nat and Rekha are here, too, so we'll have all three brothers for a . . . a nice get-together." She sounded harried.

This was the first time the Learys hadn't had Christmas at the folks' sagging home in Waterville. Tad, Nat, and Les had all relocated to the New York area, and Dad's heart attack had sig-naled to all that it was time to regroup for this year's Annual Report. When Christmas shifts from the aging parents' home to that of the child with the biggest house, it's the passing of the torch, a shift of capitals and empires, like the Roman Empire or the papal seat shifting, from Rome to Avignon or Byzantium, from New York to Washington, D. C., from the Old World to the New.

"I look forward to it," Tad responded, unsure if he should violate Bonny's policy of cheerfulness. "How's Les today?"

"He's all right," she said, though Tad could sense her tension. Facing bankruptcy, Les had attempted shooting himself, only to have the bullet pass lightly through his brain's frontal lobe, not lobotomizing him exactly, but leaving him unusually tranquil for a zealous chief executive. "He's not in pain or anything, and that's what's important. In fact, right now he's taking a nap. Listen, you know his birthday is Wednesday, whether or not he does."

"Oh, right!" Les was eight years older than Tad, and to Tad the child, pragmatic teen Les had always been remarkably free of bitterness about having his birthday eclipsed by Christmas rowdydow. Les never brooded like Tad; he loved working the present. "I almost forgot!"

"I know it's dumb, but I made a cake for him, and it looks like there aren't any birthday candles here."

"You want me to bring some?"

"Would you please?"

"No problem. I'll be there right around eleven."

Tad remembered he hadn't done any shopping for family gifts, and his two small nephews might expect presents even though the holy day was a few days off. They were too young to be gracious if they didn't like what they got, and their playtime obsessions changed almost weekly, so Tad decided to gather clues at brunch and choose presents after that.

Last Christmas, he had made a point of not getting Angelo a gift—it had been his passive way of provoking the breakup he'd thought he wanted. It had worked, the way shooting Archduke Ferdinand brought on the war, but now he regretted his backhandedness. He tried to change his mental channel as his inner closed-circuit aired, just for him, Angelo's confused, wet-eyed expression, the second annual broadcast of *A Special Awful Christmas*.

Tad considered heading downtown on his bicycle, but the television had forecast snow, and he didn't want to pedal home at midnight in a blizzard. He grabbed his black leather jacket, which he'd gotten after the breakup to boost his sense of power, even though he'd been disconcerted when his middle brother, Nat, had seen it in September and said, "Is that your gay uniform?" In puerile, macho defiance of recently rough Fate, he took no gloves or hat. In old Irish songs, the suitor stands hatless in the rain outside his sweetheart's, dies as a result, and is lionized for doing so.

In the small vestibule of the building, he saw on the table for errant junk mail a charity solicitation from the American Cancer Society aimed at one of his neighbors who had just died of the disease. Planned Parenthood had sent Tad a booklet, also unnecessarily, and there were a few unclaimed catalogs for clothes and holiday cheese wheels. Again, Tad felt remiss for not yet having done his Christmas shopping, and again he criticized his self-criticism, since he still had four days to do it, and most humans procrastinate.

He emerged onto the still side street, with Riverside Drive's low stone wall and ceiling of frail branches a few yards away. Technically, he was living on West Eighty-fourth, but he preferred to refer to it by its honorific, Edgar Allan Poe Street. Given the choice between math and English, statistic and mythology, Tad took the latter. Taxi drivers, of course, never knew where Edgar Allan Poe Street was, so Tad sometimes had to submit to the gridwork terminology.

After being indoors all weekend like an animal eluding hunters, he was surprised by the toothachy cold, and the sense that the now-leafless city was draining from full color to black and white. From the park he heard several birds chirping, unexpected on a December morning, and the sounds struck him as anomalous, scraps of inappropriate happiness, like God doodling on a gray pad. Then he remembered how brother

Nat had explained to him as a boy that birds never sang out of happiness, despite the saccharine animated cartoons that depicted it that way, but to stake territorial claims or to conduct mating rituals. The animal kingdom was not about happiness. He also noticed on the sidewalk a hopscotch court sketched in chalk, and was struck that in his preoccupation he hadn't seen it there before. There were no children in his building.

"Admiring my handiwork?" He looked up, to see one of his neighbors, tired-looking but good-natured public school teacher Estelle, her long dark hair in unfamiliar braids. She was forty, but the braids made her look like a sleep-deprived teenager.

"Estelle! You drew this? For your students?" Tad now wondered whether he could survive teaching in a public school, and respected her for doing it.

"No, no, it was a *folly*!" She was a southern girl who relished unusual vocabulary. "I'd been thinking about my childhood in Mobile, as opposed to my nowhood! Christmas does that, I guess! And, I thought I'd try to reenact some part of it to see if I could get a Proustian bliss fix out of it!"

"And . . ." Tad was unnerved by an idea he would have stooped to if he'd thought of it. "How'd it work?"

"Lord!" she exclaimed, turning up her Alabama accent. Tad noticed she made it into two syllables, as in *lowered the boom*. "Tad—hopscotch is *exercise*. And not just the jumping—the drawing with chalk on my hands and knees got me winded, too! But I can throw the stone with more accuracy now. Isn't that just adulthood for you? More accuracy but less energy!"

"And does that explain the sudden braids, too?"

"No!" She blushed. "I'm going to see my ex-husband. He's in town for the holidays. He used to love me in braids! I think he liked the fantasy of deflowering a schoolgirl!" It was merry to her, or she played it that way, but it gave Tad shivers after his

Excelsior scandal. Why would Estelle bother? he wondered. Did she expect a reconciliation?

"Well . . . I hope . . ." He was going to say "it works," but decided she might not have actual seduction in mind. "I hope you have a good time!"

"Do you ever see your Mr. Silvarini?" she asked, her southern inquisitude mixing affection, gossip, and love of history. Estelle had never even met Angelo, but she seemed to take an interest in others' romantic disasters, as if cataloging them might give her some handy insight.

Tad was flustered, ashamed to admit he didn't even know if Angelo was still in New York. "Um . . . well . . ."

"Greetings, neighbors!"

It was the first-floor tenant, beefy sixtyish black trumpet player Roscoe, whose last name Tad had forgotten and kept meaning to double-check on the junk-mail table. He wore an old-fashioned porkpie hat, and looked vigorous enough to go sixteen bars without taking a breath.

"Sunday in New York!" Roscoe said with forced but effective geniality, and Tad wondered if that was the title of a jazz standard.

"Roscoe! Brunch-bound?" Tad played All's Well When It Isn't as well as any New Yorker.

"Yes, but not to mine. I got three gigs today. This is the apex of *The Christmas Party Zone!*" Roscoe carried his trumpet case in one hand and a bulky suit carrier over his shoulder. "After all this celebration, I'm goin' to need a vacation."

"Oh, well . . . Keep a-goin'!" Estelle drawled, apparently quoting some childhood verse that Tad couldn't place.

"It's not all *biz-niss,*" Roscoe drawled back at her. "I'm seein' my son later."

"Your son!" Subletter Tad knew next to nothing about his neighbors. "I didn't know you had—I mean, have a son!"

Roscoe was clearly proud. "He just passed me in height. He'll vote for the next president."

Estelle, too, seemed uninformed, and she lived here. "You're, uh, divorced, Roscoe?"

Roscoe shrugged. "Well, it's not that simple." A world where divorce is what's simple is a complicated world. To change the subject, he turned to Tad. "Are you still workin' on that heaven thing?"

"Aren't we all?"

"I mean that book or whatever you were writing. I told you, I've got a lot of old gospel songs on seventy-eights with some mighty *unique heavens*." Roscoe half-sang a few bars, lightly, and it reminded Tad of his grandmother speed-speaking through a hectic rosary. "'You don't have to look swell, not for this hotel . . .' And there's one about life as a baseball game where Satan pitches and Jesus is the catcher, waitin' to welcome you Home. And of course there's righteous High Struttin' heaven, puttin' on a crown and walkin' around."

"Seventy-eights! Roscoe, I don't even have a turntable. I mean, Garth doesn't." Tad felt sheepish that he was a man without means, a wayfarer.

"I got one. Come down after the holidays are out of the way. We'll do gin and Jesus!" Roscoe called over his shoulder as he headed up the block toward West End Avenue. It didn't seem like a convenient moment for Tad to tell him he'd no longer be there after the holidays.

"The weather report says heavy snow later!" Estelle said, fitting a pair of earmuffs on her head like a pilot readying for takeoff. There'd been no real snow yet in the season, though there'd been some halfhearted meandering dandruff the day before. "You need a hat, young man! You'll freeze to death!" She headed toward Riverside Drive as Tad paused, unsure if she was being funny or if she had unconsciously slipped into teacher mode for a few seconds.

He decided to stick with his hatlessness, and set out to seek his fortune.

2. Who's Who in Purgatory

A candy wrapper blew across his path as Tad crossed West End Avenue. When he saw candy wrappers on the sidewalk, or when he saw used condoms floating in the Hudson River, part of Tad invariably reflected that someone had had candy and he hadn't. Another part of him would then point out he'd been spared excess calories or squalor.

In two short blocks, he went from the thoughtful still life of Riverside Drive to the rattling midway kineticism of Broadway, his second reenactment of birth trauma that morning. As he reached Eighty-sixth and Broadway to enter the subway, and birdsong was succeeded by auto horns and exhaust, Tad glimpsed in the shadows under some construction scaffolding a homeless man asleep on his cartful of unredeemed soda cans—which to Tad, who could bear reality only by dressing it in metaphor, evoked a bargain-basement Norse troll guarding his treasure. Could that be me in six months? he wondered. One of his mother's uncles had been a bum, the old pejorative for homeless, so Tad knew that genetically, he had it in him. He just hoped he could be homeless indoors.

The subway station's token booth bulletin board usually featured cheerful daily axioms like "The Chinese words for *crisis* and *opportunity* are the same word" or "Honor is bestowed, but pride you give yourself." However, in recent weeks, the messages had started to take on a disturbing edge, like "Love is as invisible as air" and "When you fall into her arms, you fall into her hands." This morning, the wobbly Magic-Marker lines were, "It is as important to express anger as it is hate." He wondered if the employee who posted these slogans were himself having a crisis.

"Um, excuse me," Tad asked the bored-looking clerk as he bought several tokens. "Who writes those sayings?" He cocked his head to indicate the bulletin board.

The clerk shrugged. "I don't know, kid. Somebody on the night shift. I'm too busy for that. You just go on along now."

There were people in line behind Tad, so he took the, as always, patronizing hint and proceeded to drop his token into the turnstile and leave this research project to others. Once again, he'd been mistaken for a child. It was a family curse. All three Leary boys were short, and despite their short father's eternal invocations of bantam boxers, feisty jockeys, and Saint James of the Bowery—the family name for Jimmy Cagney—everyone secretly knew smallness was a disadvantage.

Les had used Napoléon, Mike Todd, and the many eighties Wall Street midget moguls as his role models. He enacted the fireplug wrestler in high school, won the debating prize, and then became a pit bull in the sales world. Like polio survivors who become champion skaters, he rose in the ranks to CEO, a title that makes an individual sound like a robot you can't kill, or, worse, a corporation. But even chief executives can't be made crackproof as part of their perks.

Middle brother Nat had gone into natural science, as if to figure out nature and then take revenge on it. He had specialized in studying social orders in domesticated wild animals like elephants and yaks, to whom his height was immaterial, and in any case outside their sphere of judgment, insofar as livestock have judgment. Conversely, in another study, some poultry had mistaken Nat for their mother, proving that, in nature, human shortness is more relative.

As if to round out the curriculum, tertiary Tad, sequentially the baby, had gravitated to fine arts, forgetting *fine* can mean "extremely limited" and "narrow." Literature wasn't a job, but at least there was no dangerous machinery involved. He had taken refuge from mankind in the humanities. Tad's affinity for folktales, where the youngest of three sons always wins in the end, led him to immerse himself in it for consolation. Still, smallness, like poverty, is a virtue only in fantasies.

The subway train arrived almost immediately, which Tad interpreted as a wink from God, promising at least trivial relief from his travails. As it headed to Times Square, Tad contemplated the advertisements aimed at its captives:

HAVE YOU BEEN INJURED?

DOMESTIC VIOLENCE IS EVERYBODY'S BUSINESS.

CURE WARTS WITH LASER SURGERY.

LEARN A TRADE.

DO YOU HAVE LUPUS?

STOP SMOKING COMFORTABLY.

Tad wondered if that last ad offered to teach you how to start smoking *un*comfortably. As a litany, the ads reminded Tad that he moved in a different realm than glossy Dean Parish, who'd been his lover only momentarily, like a man-made element that blazes into being for just a fraction of a second. Dean edited a local society magazine full of advertisements for pearl necklaces, co-ops whose monthly maintenance fee could buy a house in Waterville, and financial security packages whose functioning Tad couldn't even grasp. It was called *Vision,* but it didn't seem to see anything that existed west of Fifth Avenue or north of Ninety-sixth, except for an occasional squint southward to Palm Beach. Tad hadn't even enjoyed Dean's stolid company, but he had mistaken Dean's mannequin composure and sheen as an improvement on Angelo's gauche Italian effusiveness. Tad shivered, a reluctant troglodyte, and noticed another provocatively worded ad overhead, floating like a visitation:

DIVORCE YOURSELF FOR FIFTY DOLLARS.

If only you could get divorced from yourself, he thought. His body was an unwelcome partner to him, the lamp confining his genie, and Tad, in his mad, glad sadness, had never felt so confused.

Across the aisle, he sighted a smooth-faced young beauty, crew-cut and decent in a blue hiker's parka. That hopeful college boy is my ideal, he mused, only to realize as she turned her head that this ideal was a young woman. It was the third time in less than a month he had made such a mistake, and Tad was bewildered that even his desires were contradictory. He assumed the rest of the world knew its heart's desire, whether or not they got it, but he didn't get it in either sense. Women were beautiful and smooth, but complex and hidden, and in the clinch, he was frightened. Men were familiar, but coarse and unavailing, and he didn't want them so much as he wanted to become them. To Tad, facial hair on others was repulsive; it seemed an evolutionary graffito. Chimpanzees didn't have facial hair, so why should men? Unexpectedly, he thought of Saint Wilgefortis and the soldier in his *Lives of the Medieval Saints* who recoiled when the saintly female virgin he was pursuing sprouted a beard after she prayed to God for help in fending him off. Even the milk mustaches on the busty supermodels in magazine ads gave Tad an uneasy feeling.

His few partners, however, except for Angelo, had all been larger and darker than he was, and he'd felt strangely as though he were after their pelts, that he was Dan'l Boone killing their b'ar. He'd clutch and gnaw at them like a jealous cannibal, trying to conquer or acquire their essences, usually picking up only the barbiturate of their personal problems, the draining equivalent of their mad-cow viruses. At this point, though, exhausted by the irrational equation, Tad's theory was, If there's no conception possible, why bother? Sex was beautiful in fantasy but risky and ridiculous in practice. Besides—hadn't he slept with the most beautiful girl at Hale? On the third hand, he contradicted himself, hadn't he slept with her for the same reason he'd slept with men later, in order to gain some status by proximity? What he didn't grasp was that it was his own selfishness that kept him lonely.

He certainly was uninterested in others' satisfaction. His agenda was only his own gratification, the phallic "I." Angelo had been no competitor, with his dangling, misplaced baby toe, like a putto's, a comma where an exclamation point is expected, but that relativity, of course, had made Tad king of their household, Zeus, hurler of thunderbolts. To his compartmentalized shame, Tad had never felt in his heart that he loved Angelo, but he'd known Angelo loved him, and that had made him safe and comfortable for five years. Angelo and grad school were to be temporary hiding places. He could bide his time, work on his master's and then his doctoral thesis while Angelo praised him and did the cooking and cleaning, first in their Waterville basement and then in the Village studio he'd guiltily surrendered in the breakup.

Tad had welcomed being the relatively rugged realist in their partnership. Angelo was so foolishly good, he chased after tourists on the street when he felt his directions to them had been unclear, and he agonized that he couldn't oblige the telemarketers who darkened the dinner hour. He fretted over ailing potted plants like they were E.T. on the operating table, and tiptoed through any room where a cat or dog was sleeping. He smiled reflexively at anyone whose gaze he met, a mixture of friendliness and fear that Tad had found disarming initially but later came to see as craven, like a chimpanzee's appeasement grin.

Tad was remorseful now, remembering fellow townie Angelo as the most unreconstructed of old-fashioned wives, all the time singing in his innocently overbearing off-key Boston accent the show tunes Tad found so inane. He admired Angelo's purity for belting out "Home on the Range" without irony while washing dishes, but he was maddened when Angelo got song lyrics mixed up, like "the clouds are not cloudy at all," or "Whistling words of wisdom / Let it be." Still, Angelo, younger and, uniquely, smaller, had worshiped Tad as the seeker who'd risen in the ranks and become a great Hale graduate—or else he stoically pretended to, geisha-style, and avowed his submissive adulation to Tad with the intensity only a man would wish for in his idealized partner. Now, Tad didn't even know where Angelo was.

In the dank clamor of the Times Square station, where, like Hades, no sense of Sunday could ever permeate, Tad passed a bizarrely robed swarthy man with a handful of leaflets, arguing with a pale bald man who wore earrings in both ears. "It's not *me* who hates them!" he heard the leafleteer saying. "It's *God* who hates them!" Tad was tempted to fish one of the discarded leaflets out of the trash barrel he saw just yards ahead, but at the last minute he resisted. If it was him God hated, Tad didn't want to know. He remembered a few years ago, as he stood on a subway platform, a passing lunatic had seen him momentarily appraise the covers of the men's fashion magazines. In one of those intuitive leaps that lunatics make without hesitation, the stranger had growled, "AIDS gonna get you!" Tad was left shaking, not from the threat of future illness, but the threat of present hatred.

The crosstown shuttle was crowded with people who had tacitly agreed not to acknowledge one another's existence. Tad sat opposite a tired teenaged mother whose hyperactive toddler daughter was fascinated by the tunnel's passing lights and who knelt on the jiggling seat to watch them wheel past like ball lightning. "Sit down." The mother repositioned her brusquely. "How many times I tell you not to be looking at things?"

Tad's eyes met those of a young black nurse with a Bible, also opposite him. It struck him as odd that a person of science would also carry a virtual *grimoire* of magic spells, but he then had to admit that people who get up early to work on Sundays with the dying probably need reserves of spiritual strength. She subtly rolled her eyes at Tad, in secret conspiratorial annoyance at this dubious parenting, the same way his mom often would to Tad at wedding receptions when groggy Dad started blowing hard on conversational tangents she was apparently helpless to stop. For a moment, Tad felt connected to mankind, and, furthermore, he wished he could be that girl's father, and tell her, "Yes, delight in those lights! The world is full of variations of light—sunset and *Kugelblitz* and will-o'-the-wisp and aurora borealis and the luminescent tiny portholes on those deep-sea fishes! Go ahead and look! As far as I can see, that's what life is for!" On the other hand, he didn't have to change her diapers or endure her tantrums, not to mention take her to see Santa, or whatever labor the tired mom was indirectly complaining about.

The escalator ride to street level seemed exceptionally long to Tad, inevitably reminding him of the escalator in cartoons that takes people up to heaven, or abruptly, should the rider think something impious, converts to a slide to hell. Ahead of him were two leering high school boys in hockey caps, and as they neared the top, Tad overheard the end of a joke one was telling the other. ". . . So the elephant turns around and says to the ant, 'What are you doing back there?' and the ant says, 'Take it all, bitch!'" His companion groaned rather than laughed, and they and Tad fell silent in the general noise as they completed their ascent.

He crossed the great hall of Grand Central Station, its sea green vaulted ceiling, salted with constellations, playing sky for a miniature world below. Beneath its false welkin, thousands of horoscopes besides his hurried to their daily opportunities and risks.

The cold air on Lexington Avenue was harsh but refreshing, official proof that he had left the Underworld. He headed uptown and east, where skyscrapers shone even in the gray light like phalluses in shiny novelty condoms or extra-large bottles of caffeinated soda. In one of the vast corporate lobbies Tad passed he saw, instead of a Christmas tree, a single house-sized Christmas tree bulb, a joke like the pointlessly world's largest chair Tad had seen in North Carolina once, promoting the local furniture makers. The huge red bulb, shiny as the sky-scraper and the profits it generated, inexplicably irritated Tad. It was like the obese prizewinning pumpkins or monstrous pigs the newspapers featured at harvest time, or the mile-long submarine sandwich unveiled as a photo op—a celebration of bigness as bestness, of *The Guinness Book of World Records* outweighing the Bible. Godzilla was an accountant's idea of horror—by the yard—and was less frightening to Tad than a tarantula. He figured, We can all see Godzilla coming, so the suspense is minimal. Even the Macy's parade had been lost on him as a child. There was clever little Snoopy, only it was an enormous, palpably lifeless version of him. Childe Tad, watching the tiny TV image of the gargantuan crude rubber balloon versions of the small platonically imaginary characters, had wondered, *And?* What's the point? What do we learn? To him, humans in Mickey Mouse costumes were all wrong—wrongly fuzzy, wrongly huge, preposterous imposters without even the wit to speak, and, most of all, wrong in their very three-dimensionality. Likewise, the face of God in paintings was never fabulous enough. God with a human face was God wearing a stupid mask.

Far more interesting to him even back then was the notion of miniaturization, and he'd avidly overseen his collection of tiny jungle animals, of tiny knights in combat, of perfect Train Town citizens he could crush. He had been their God then, holding each in the palm of his hand. Besides, miniaturized, they were now comprehensible; immobilized, they had limits. In a child's bedroom, the universe need not be infinite, and therefore not frightening.

Tad walked to Les and Bonny's town house on East Fifty-fifth Street. This place alone would have satisfied most pelf-seekers, but it was merely their pied-à-terre, for business trips. They had two other homes, one in a gated community in suburban Whitehaven, the other a beach house down in Apogee, on the Gulf Coast. Tad assumed that since the financial collapse of the nationwide chain of VitaManager stores—where busy executives could buy bottles of vitamins at drive-through windows, and which Les had pioneered and controlled—not to mention the subsequent collapse of Les, some or all of those addresses might be in jeopardy. Tad rang the doorbell.

"Who is it?" Bonny's voice reverberated like a kazoo through the intercom.

Her remoteness frustrated Tad. "Um . . . It's a serial killer. Are there at least two people there? Come on, Bonny! I said I'd arrive at eleven, and it's eleven! Open the door!"

There was a pause. The cold gripped Tad like an unwanted lover. "Who is it, please?" Bonny had gone security-mad since moving out to their Whitehaven compound. She had always imagined New York as a prime-time TV drama of gunfire and relentless violation, and now, especially since Les's accident, she had to cling to any security system available. Les had always joked that in the limo after their wedding, she'd locked the doors to keep him from escaping, but Tad theorized that actually she didn't like the look of the shabby Waterville streets they were riding through.

Tad surrendered. "It's Tad, Bonny."

Over the intercom, Tad heard Bonny chastising her rambunctious five-year-old. "No, Hunter! I said no! I think it's time for a time-out!" The name Hunter had been her idea of classy, even though scientist Nat had teasingly told her she should next have a daughter and name her Gatherer.

"Bonny?" He pressed the doorbell one more time.

"Oh, sorry!" Bonny buzzed him in.

As Tad walked down the hall toward the parlor-floor apartment, he heard the off-puttingly familiar cadences of his already-tipsy father. When Dad drank, he inevitably waxed, or rather, waned sentimental about his childhood poverty. "My dad used to beat the crap out of me when I goofed up!" he was saying. "That got me in line. No time-outs, let me tell you. But I suppose today they'd call that *child abuse.*"

"Well, yes, of course, they would, certainly!" Nat's wife Rekha's barely suppressed impatience with Dad could be felt even through the wood door, even though her musical Indian voice strained to conceal it. Tad tried the doorknob. That door, too, was locked.

"Bonny, is this hall a decontamination chamber or something? Open the door!"

"I wanna get it! I wanna get it!" he heard Hunter shout right on the other side.

"All right, you'll have to learn to receive people sometime!" Bonny said.

The door opened, and there in the vestibule was tiny milk-blond trophy child Hunter, wide-eyed, scared and motionless, the kindergartner with stage fright. He had forgotten that opening the door entailed socializing afterward.

"Hunter! Hey!" Tad greeted him as brightly and unintimidatingly as he could, although he was inwardly frustrated at being forgotten in the few months since he'd last seen the boy.

"Hunter, you recognize your uncle Tad!" Bonny appeared in a red sweater that featured a winking snowman's head. Her tone was arch, but she then reverted to a normal voice. "He's like this with the telephone, too. He's crazy eager to answer it, but then he's terrified to speak into it!"

In his hand, Hunter held a slice of baloney, which he had folded in half and taken one bite from, so it had a seemingly impossible nibble at its center.

"I like that trick bite in your baloney!" Tad tried to engage him. "You could do two bites and make a sort of baloney mask!"

Hunter complied expressionlessly, and took another bite of the folded lunch meat. He held the makeshift mask to his face, and his eyes now glittered through the openings. Tad saw his own interested, reticent self in those glittering eyes. If Tad and Les shared half the same genetic material, and Hunter had half of Les's, Tad figured, then Hunter was one quarter the same person as himself.

Hunter tilted his head back so the baloney would remain on his face without his holding it, then paraded back into the living room and out of sight. Dad could be heard telling the one about how his father had never seen a banana until they handed them out to the detained newcomers on Ellis Island.

"Don't hide in the bedroom forever!" Bonny called after Hunter. "I want you and Little Nat to come and join the grown-ups!" She turned back to Tad and added confidentially, "All the beautiful buffet in there, and that's all he'll eat. Come on in. I'll take your jacket." She hugged Tad minimally, which made him wonder if she considered his gayness strange, or whether she assumed all others, not just him, were strangers to be approached warily. He remembered that when he'd waltzed with her at her wedding, she'd positioned her body at a right angle to his, rather than face-to-face, to separate their bodies— the choreographic equivalent of twin beds. But then, he pointed out to himself, attempting to be fair, that may have been appropriate for a bride.

Tad followed Bonny into the living room. It was furnished with beautiful leather upholstery and elaborate window treatments, as Bonny would have referred to them. The bankruptcy proceedings were presumably going to affect all this. Tad thought of the tale of "The Fisherman's Wife"—how Les and Bonny had started out in the upstairs of a drab Waterville duplex, and how Bonny, feral and instinctive like her mate, had gone through half a dozen ever-larger houses as Les rose in the world, decorating each to a fare-thee-well and then saying fare thee well to it. She avidly read magazines like *Modern Shelter, Abode Options,* and *Better Domiciles,* which didn't even offer the happy finality of depicting the best, simply the ever-ascending better, a tantalizing spiral that left its consumer hungrier than before. Tad recalled she once had a room in the Whitehaven house redecorated for a party because her guests had "already seen it." Now she was sliding backward through the story, into ever-smaller quarters, back to the fisherman's barrel, and she was struggling with assimilating the rewrites. She and Tad were more similar than either knew at that moment.

In the adjacent dining room, Tad glimpsed the table invitingly laid with a miniature plastic sleigh of fruit salad, a carefully stacked Aztec-style pyramid of doughnuts, a glass-covered platter of scrambled eggs and bacon, steaming like a shoppe window of yesteryear, cold cuts laid out like a shingled roof in a kiddie book, and a velvet-trimmed treasure chest–shaped basket intentionally overspilling with Christmas cookies, including a related tray of gingerbread folk. Bonny still managed and innovated, despite her upheavals, Tad conceded, and he acknowledged, to his own discredit, how in his comparably lesser trials he'd eaten cold gravy from a can and let dirty dishes pile up in Garth's sink.

The impersonally tasteful Xmas tree Bonny had set up—it was an Xmas tree, not a Christmas tree—had uniform tiny red balls on it, none of the piquant menagerie of accumulated cheap treasure with which most families trim their trees. Tad thought momentarily of the tarnished diversity of the ornaments Dad and Mom had hauled down annually from the Waterville attic. Christmas ornaments are as close as most regular families ever get to an art collection. He recalled the oddities on the family tree—the peekaboo pendant quasi–Easter egg with the Holy Family hunkering inside, the salacious cherries oddly glazed with frost, the seeming miniature disco ball with its mirrored facets like a fly's eye, the strange elongated glass icicles like uselessly fragile drill bits, the crummy mandala of Popsicle sticks Les had made in kindergarten, the shimmering purple onion-shaped Turkish domes some unaccountably fancy relative must have donated.

Tad braced himself, despite an interior rash of uneasiness, and entered the arena. As with life, he pined for his family but then had the urge to flee in their midst. "Hello, all! God bless us, everyone! This message void where prohibited by law." Tad tried to make fun of his cute image so it couldn't be used against him like surprise evidence in court. He reflected that, whatever his humiliations, at least he had escaped playing Tiny Tim onstage. Oliver Twist was a roughneck by comparison.

"Tad! You made it safe!" Mom greeted him plaintively, combining goodwill with a sense of constant danger. She was a tiny sparrow, as short Dad's pride had required his bride to be, and she saw life as an antechamber where you wait for the X-ray results.

Dad, grizzly, ruddy, smelling of tobacco, glass in hand, greeted Tad with "Well! It's the elf himself!" Dad was very funny at press conferences, but unfortunately, that's what he conducted even at home.

"Hey, Dad!" *Hey* is somehow less commital than *hi*. Tad knew Dad teased him about his height the way bald men tease one another, from a mixed sense of solidarity and self-consciousness.

"Ah! The homunculus has arrived." Tad heard Nat's monotone from elsewhere in the room. "I'd say 'the dwarf,' but I have to admit, his limbs are perfectly proportioned." Nat was only an inch taller than Tad, but just as Tad had dominated five-foot Angelo by a mere inch, so five-two Nat worked his advantage over his little brother. Besides, Nat had had to go to a city college, whereas Tad had luckily been accepted at Hale, and Nat had to assert his superiority somehow, despite that status destabilizer. The old cartoons of an infinite sequence of fish swallowing their inferior, while being swallowed in turn, flashed through Tad's mind.

Then he saw Nat was in a leather armchair, off in a corner.

"You know, the short joke wears thin after about thirty years," Tad recited.

"Not if it still bugs you!" his older brother countered.

Nat was gazing deep into a palm-top computer he'd brought with him from the suburbs. It glowed like a cauldron in use, and gave messy-bearded Nat a warlock's lit-from-beneath face. He stared into his crystal not like Nostradamus or Narcissus, but impassively, his fingers benignly click-clicking on the keyboard as if he were deploying knitting needles. Tad thought of the old war movies, where the submarine ensign concentrates not on the room he's in, but on the radar screen, intent on some revelation of danger or treasure elsewhere. Nat had grown more and more detached with the years. His occasional beard was grown initially to counteract his short-ness (he didn't use the wildly obvious but nonetheless preva-lent cigar ploy the way business honcho Les had, and Les in turn had nixed bearddom as borderline Bolshevik, unaccept-able to his Bible Belt customers), but it also recurred because he tired of superfluous niceties like daily shaving. Tad won-dered if it was a hedge grown for privacy, to keep the world at a more clinical distance. He wondered if it kept Rekha away as well, but where attraction is concerned, one man's moot is another man's passion. It must have taken all autumn to raise that beard, on that research project in shaving-not-required Africa, Tad thought, given the sparsity of the Leary cheek. In a way, Tad felt he'd been the bravest Leary son, at least in this instance, remaining uncompensatingly clean-shaven and cigar-free, even though it meant being mistaken for a child.

Tad greeted his brother by his high school nickname. "Good ol' Nat Sci! The mad zookeeper! You brought your computer to brunch?" Its showy standoffishness reminded him of Nat's teenage rebellion period, when he'd worn his Walk-man at the dinner table to bypass family interaction. Mom had said it was like feeding the living dead, and Dad had said at least the living dead didn't have tuition expenses.

"One of them," Nat answered, with ostentatious flatness. He had an array of computers, small and large, though Tad never comprehended what one did that another couldn't.

"Ah!" Tad offered approval, hoping for the same in return. "Your desk away from desk."

"He says he has work to do," Mom said tartly. "God forbid we should have a decent conversation."

"Just answering some E-mail," Nat said without looking up. "I'm in a news group. We're discussing how to use the pro-gram we're using to discuss the program we're using."

Tad tried to connect with his brother by making a joke. Dad and Les had never paid any attention to him—they were hopeless projects—but Nat, only three years older, at one time had been his partner in ridiculing the larger world. "Some-times I think you care more about your little noncorporeal on-line friends than you do about me!" He pretended to sob.

"You sound like a certain wife I know," Nat responded emotionlessly.

Tad didn't dare look over to wherever Rekha was for her take on this. When she disapproved of something, her voice remained soft, but her eyes darkened like Kali about to cleanse the earth of itself.

"Enough with the typing already!" Dad carped humorously. "Typing is for weekdays and women!" In Dad's days at the mayor's office, men didn't type; they dictated.

Nat finally looked up to meet Tad's gaze. "Yikes, what happened to you? You look like Snap or Crackle after the rottweiler got to him."

Tad felt a knot in his stomach. Nat always acted playful, but his tactless gibes sometimes had an edge of redirected frustration. Nat was having job trouble, too, and although he never talked about his marital happiness, his and Rekha's careers kept them apart for strenuous periods of time.

"I haven't slept too well lately," Tad offered tersely.

"Whoa, and what's that on your chin? Have you been eating barbecue potato chips?"

"I didn't shave. Sunday simplicity." Tad tried to change the subject. "I like your natty wardrobe!" Nat was wearing blue jeans and a white button-down shirt, just like Tad. "How was Africa?"

"Corrupt and bankrupt. My project was basically poached out of existence."

Tad, meanwhile, saw his mother was watching him, waiting to be greeted. Outside their own home, parental protocol and privilege become ambiguous.

"I think you already know the Judge and the Drudge?" Nat feigned the manners of the grand ballroom as he gestured to his parents, who were sitting in perpetually floral armchairs by the room's bay window.

"Hey, Ma, Hey again, Dad," Tad said. Nonchalance is confused love's best opening gambit.

"*¡Feliz Navidad!*" Dad joked, as if wishing happy holidays in English was too emotional for him.

"Good to see you," Mom said. "I worry about you!" Tad inwardly flinched. *I love you in spite of that.* If wedding announcements were worded *"John XY will be inserting his engorged penis into the vagina of Mary XX,"* he thought, wouldn't heterosexuality seem scarifying, as well? It's the visualizing that frightens people.

"When did you all get in?" Tad inquired ritualistically.

"Yesterday afternoon." Mom said. There was a snag of silence before conscious social improvisation could kick in. Tad noticed the television opposite the couch was on, but with the sound turned off, and its shifting light played on the walls and faces like pale blue firelight.

"And . . . how's Les?" As a teacher, Tad was used to inducing conversation.

"He walks and talks and everything," Dad began, mustering his old spin control. "He even seems—what's the word? *Relaxed*. But I don't see him flying jumbo jets anytime soon."

Mom added her diagnosis. "He's asleep. For the moment, I mean. Though in a larger sense, too, I suppose. . . . When I think of what *might* have happened, I just thank the Lord he's still with us." Her own brother, a longshoreman, had been killed by a falling crate of machine parts. Tad was born after his death, and he could never visualize his unknown uncle's end without a guilty twinge of cartoon amusement.

"Now, Midge . . ." Dad's voice of consolation had an edge of reprimand in it.

Tad tried to keep the proceedings upbeat. "Hi, Rekha! Getting some candid footage of *Leary-us americanus*?"

Nat's petite wife was a freelance nature photographer. She'd met Nat in Bombay when he was a graduate assistant on a study of the effects of pollution on elephants in urban workplaces. She sat in a rocker by the couch, but her poise, like a temple idol's, was such that the rocker didn't move. "Hey, I like *your* wardrobe!" Tad joked. Rekha, too, wore blue jeans and a crisp white shirt. "We're the College Crowd Coffee Bar Singers!" Rekha was thoughtful and slow to speak, so some Leary or other usually interrupted her.

"She's going from here to spend Christmas on a shoot for *National Photogenic*—at the North Pole!" Mom announced with awe, since Rekha did things no woman Mom knew in her childhood would have been allowed to do. Mom had wanted to study music, but she was forced into taking shorthand. Tad remembered that he had noticed Rekha's camera equipment and some luggage piled in the vestibule.

"I hope it pays well!" Dad said.

"Away from your son on Christmas!" Mom seemed to be reciting a headline about a bus plunge. "Science can be so cold!"

"Especially in this case!" Dad leapt in triumphantly, staking his comedy claim before his competitive heirs could.

"Insert Santa's workshop jokes here. I guess." Tad smiled at Rekha.

"Don't even start," Nat mumbled from his corner. "That kind of corn rolls off Rekha like water off an alpha duck." Nat had once studied a flock of wild ducks to see how the alpha duck was determined. Somehow, they'd accidentally picked him, and the study had to be abandoned.

"Alpha duck," Tad mused. "It sounds like a parody of a superhero."

"It's a fact of nature," Nat answered. His adolescent drollness had dried into brittleness. Tad could remember when Nat had energetically enjoyed himself. Nat had been a prankish teen, and at one school talent show, he sang a cowboy spoof with words he wrote himself, surprising for a thirteen-year-old.

> *Oh my Darwin, Oh my Darwin,*
> *Oh my Darwin, man alive!*
> *I'll be lost and gone forever*
> *If I'm not fit to survive!*
>
> *In a cavern, in a canyon,*
> *Excavation Number Nine—*
> *Found some fossils of a monkey—*
> *Oh m' God, those bones are mine!*

Nat had worn a cowboy hat and a lab coat to perform the skit, and of course had gotten in trouble with the Catholic staff for saying "Oh, m' God," never mind the implicit doubts about creationism. To ten-year-old Tad, Nat had seemed the coolest.

Rekha smirked mirthlessly, as if watching something happening blocks away through a telescope, and spoke for the first time. "All males are a parody of a superhero."

Tad wondered if she was thinking of her childhood, and all the bumbling male-dominated hierarchies of the caste system. Mom had been confused at meeting Rekha, with her fathomless stare and caramel complexion. A black woman might have panicked Mom, but as she'd whispered to Tad at the couple's wedding reception, "She's not exactly Oriental even—so I don't know if this is sideways motion or what." Hindus had never been part of the social sequence in South Boston, where she grew up. The Irish weren't as good as the WASPs, but they certainly felt free to look down on blacks. Mom had no malice in her; she was just a rueful spectator of what prevailed. Nat may have aspired to rise to Rekha's exotic level, and maybe Rekha saw Nat as a connection to a more rational and secure Western lifestyle that would have better-equipped darkrooms. Or else both thought they were doing the other the favor, since Nat had a hard time finding short American girls who'd tolerate him disappearing for months. Like many, theirs was a mutually morganatic alliance.

"How's Sheep's Crossing?" Tad returned to Rekha, who remained composed, even as reflected images of football mayhem from the soundless television distorted her face. Nat and his family lived in a small town near the college that was sponsoring his latest studies.

"Small-minded, but we're leaving."

"Stop! Rewind! What?"

"Nat took that job at Generalized Foods."

"The chickens-in-bondage project," Nat added, a verbal footnote. "Can they live full lives without ever moving?"

"You're going to Illinois?"

"Yes, but after the North Pole, I think I'll be able to handle it," Rekha answered.

"I'll go round up the boys," Bonny said. "They're playing computer games. Tad, help yourself. There's coffee in that silver urn."

"Thanks, Bonny!" Tad called after her, and then sensed he was standing in the center of the room while everyone else sat. He went to the dining room and poured a cup of coffee for himself. "How's retirement, Dad? Taking it easy?" he called, noting that the room was silent without his efforts. Tad stirred some cream in his coffee, and the spoon clattered, the galloping hooves of approaching caffeine.

"Well, you know, I think that heart attack was nature's way of telling me to die." Dad's jokes always sounded secondhand somehow, as if he had writers hidden somewhere, just as he himself had written material for Mayor Halloran over the years. "So here's to nature's bad advice!" He made a mock toast as Tad returned, and Tad saw that his father's murky beverage was in a novelty glass that sported a skull and crossbones with *What's Your Poison?* lettered on it.

"Doesn't the genteel retiree wait until noon to hit the hard stuff?" Tad hoped he sounded raffish, but his voice was strained. He remembered liquor as his rival, as the one Dad embraced when he came home late at night from fund-raising dinners or whatever obscure policy sessions Waterville could have demanded. The only time Dad had ever mentioned him with praise was in his heavily miked retirement speech, lumped in with Nat and Les as one of the "three fine sons" he said he considered his greatest accomplishment.

Mom squirmed, an uncomfortable accessory to a crime. "It's his only pleasure. And you know your father's never done a thing he didn't want to do." Tad thought of Angelo's chain-smoking mother, who smoked even while praying, and how grief-stricken dutiful Angelo had been at her early death, and how, at the grave site on the first anniversary of her passing, her three gardener sons had all silently lit cigarettes and inserted them filter-down into the earth by her stone, temporary eternal flames. It had struck Tad as garish at first, like so many things the Silvarinis did, but then it seemed a beautiful gesture. After all, how bad could smoking be for the dead?

"Besides, the milk is supposed to make up for the whiskey," Mom added. Tad was mystified by her acquiescence to Dad's bad habits, especially after his heart attack. Has she given up? he thought. Does she secretly want him to die? Tad remembered when they used to jump on the beds, and Mom would say, "All right, keep it up, one of you will break your head open!" and Nat did. The ambulance had come to take him away, and Tad briefly respected her ability to see the future.

"He has an ulcer, too," Mom explained, as if Dad had left the room. In a way, he had.

Dad chortled to indicate he was a lovable rascal. "I don't have ulcers, I *cause* 'em!"

Nat played an eerily flat straight man. "Har har, sir," he answered dutifully, simulating an underclassman at a military academy.

Mom frowned. "Don't call your father sir," she chided. "It's disrespectful."

"If I have the whiskey mixed with milk, it's safe for my stomach," Dad protested.

Tad went back to the dining room for more coffee. "Really? Is that backed up by chemistry?"

"Certainly not by mixology," Nat called from the living room.

Dad played himself. "It's just a short stagger from a brandy Alexander." He then lit a cigarette.

"You are kidding me!" Tad came back in and overacted his surprise. After all, Dad had always smoked. "Mom, you allow this? Are the cigarettes soaked in milk, too?"

"I wish you wouldn't, Packy, around the grandchildren," Mom murmured, filing her petition with a sense of its futility. She had been raised to stand by her man or risk mortal sin, and besides, she had never driven a car or signed a check, and she defined herself through him. Waterville politics and Waterville Latin had been all about men, and Tad briefly wondered if this was why he prized male approval, not as a misfit, but as a typical member of his community. "I'm glad you don't smoke, Tad. At least you're safer there." Again, *at least.*

Hunter wandered back in, evidently following orders, but he groped along like he was playing blindman's buff. He was still leaning backward, still wearing his lunch-meat face. "How do you like my baloney mask?" He approached Nat but wasn't addressing anyone in particular.

"Sheesh, that is unsettling," Nat remarked, looking up. "It looks like the *Texas Chainsaw Massacre* guy. All he needs is the chain saw! Santa, take note!"

"Oh please," Mom protested. "Don't tempt the fates! Mrs. Hardaway down the street always joked about her little hoodlum when Liam was just a boy, and you know how he turned out!"

"Oh relax," Nat answered, his face again lowered to concentrate on his palm-top computer. "Mass murderers are blue-collar. With Hunter's social standing, he'll kill two, three people tops."

"This is a Christmas brunch," Bonny said simply, reappearing from the bedroom. "I don't want a serial killer–joke theme, all right?" She took the baloney from Hunter's face and put it on a paper plate. "Let's set this aside for later, okay, sweetie? You don't want that grease on your skin anyway."

"Look, Tad, I've built a house that's for sale!" Hunter, with the amnesiac ease of children switching activities, announced. He had constructed a little castle with Lego blocks. It looked like a typical house, except for the towers, and he had added clip-on toy machine-gun turrets on the roof. He struggled to use the adult words he had overheard. "It's a, um, *combo minimum*! We're asking one point five, but we're willing to settle for an even million!" Tad felt rattled at the child's turning his family's diminished expectations into a fantasy.

"The gun turrets are a definite selling point," Tad admitted.

Bonny looked weary. "Monkey see, monkey do. We have to sell the house in Whitehaven and, in all likelihood, the place down at Apogee. . . . This was supposed to be our *pied-à-terre*, but now it's our home, and it's really not big enough."

"Well . . ." Tad struggled to sound solicitous and not intrusive. "What's going to happen to all the VitaManager outlets?"

"What can we do? They all go in the settlement with the creditors," Bonny said, carefully keeping her voice balanced. "Those were gone before the accident." She went on for a while about Les's reckless overextension of the outlets, the terms of the bankruptcy, and the complexities of insurance, but Tad's hearing reflexively shut down, like closing the shutters on a windstorm, and he just nodded at her like the dog that sits by the dinner table, understanding nothing but its own name.

"I'm so sorry," Tad said when she was finished. Bonny had sometimes annoyed him, perhaps because she showed no interest in his folklore studies, but grief made her sympathetic. "I wish I could wave a magic wand and change things." With Nat within earshot, he instantly wished he'd used a different metaphor. Bonny wordlessly opened her palms in a gesture of either surrender or acceptance.

"Now I remember! Tad, do your thumb!" Hunter demanded, now at ease enough with his uncle to give him orders.

Tad had a double-jointed thumb, which he stretched back almost to touch his wrist. "There you go! Ta daah!"

"Excellent," Hunter pronounced, and wandered back out of the room. Besides his brevity, Tad's gymnastic thumb was his claim to sideshow stardom. Children were fascinated by it, but he made a point of concealing it from adults.

Bad luck makes slow conversation. After a dry pause like the break between movements of a symphony, Mom coughed and said cautiously, "We're going to be selling our house, too."

Tad, who had always been mortified by his modest background, who'd never invited his Hale friends to visit there, was thunderstruck. He realized he loved the house in Waterville with all his heart. He had played contentedly there, loved its chipped crannies and stained wallpaper, the shelves of torn, doleful old catechisms and fruity picture books from the Depression, and the yellowing coloring books that had already been scribbled in by Les and Nat, so to toddler Tad they looked like peaceful scenes incongruously beset by hordes of orange or green insects. He thought of the dim light that glowed in the upstairs hallway all night, the plump dust balls scudding along the floorboards like toy clouds, the flyspecked mirrors and dark green window shades, whose timeworn holes looked like planetarium constellations when light showed through them. He remembered the perennial smell of tea and greasy potatoes, of old newspaper and human hair, of fresh hot linens and pungent dirty laundry, the tang of dried sweat. He had felt safe there. Only the prospect of losing it made him understand that. When you grow up at one stable address, you have three parents—mother, father, and the house.

"What! But why?"

"Well, your father can't be expected to climb a lot of stairs now. We have to find some simple one-story place, or even an apartment, maybe out in Whitehaven, I don't know." Mom spoke the word *apartment* with distaste, since she had lived only in big old houses, and like pantsuits for grannies, such modish convenience seemed wrong to her.

"That's why the Nixons moved to Saddle River, you know," Dad said proudly, as if his heart attack was an approximation of royalty. "Pat couldn't do stairs."

"But . . ." Tad was about to point out that all his childhood toys and books were still in the attic, but he knew Nat would find that risible. For some reason, he thought again of the family's wan cardboard carton of Christmas ornaments, intentionally frangible in their old egg cartons, hope stored in Pandora's box. They'd be impossible to move without breakage. "Who's going to buy it?"

"Who knows?" Mom said, implying aborigines might squat there at any moment.

"I love that house," Tad found himself saying, and, of all things, specifically pictured Dad's forbidden liquor cabinet, and how as a child he had furtively played with the different bottles and glasses, arranging them like a futuristic city. Champagne flutes, martini glasses, wineglasses all doubled as transparent skyscrapers, and Tad had invented a whole race of imaginary mite-sized invisible telepathic beings who lived there in crystalline perfection.

Unexpectedly, Nat and Rekha's son appeared from the bedroom, where he'd been playing computer games. He was also named Nat. "It indicates the passing on of my DNA," Nat had explained at the baptism, a ceremony he and Rekha submitted to only when Mom pleaded that this might be her only grandchild, and she didn't want to die thinking the child would end up in Limbo. Now here was Little Nat, at least presumably, because his head and body were hidden under a Darth Vader headpiece and costume Tad had sent as a Halloween gift.

"He's been dressed up in that Darth Vader suit since Halloween," Bigger Nat explained. "He won't take it off. He loves the power, I guess. Watch this." He seemed to be narrating stock footage.

Little Nat ignored the company and picked up the remote control. He aimed it at the television as if it were a powerful weapon and pressed the off button. "I kill you all!" he declared as the capering humans on-screen disappeared into black emptiness, with only a receding tiny star remaining.

"I give you life!" he announced, and pressed the on but-ton. Life spontaneously regenerated on-screen. "I kill you all again!" he continued, sounding a little more casual about damnation this time, exterminating once more the broadcast figures made of shadow.

"Tohu v'bohu," Tad observed, eager to try to engage Nat. "Darkness was on the face of the deep. From nothing, some-thing. Maybe God created the universe with a big remote-control button."

Nat didn't smile, but he joked, "So everything's a big sit com—*That Darn Universe!*—and God's the couch potato who turned on the TV just to see what was on?"

Nat junior killed all life again, then grinned unseen at the minuscule central ember where the TV world had been. "I create you! I destroy you! I create you! I destroy you!" The big bang and Armageddon happened several times each.

Nat took away the remote and told Little Nat to stop. From behind his Darth Vader mask, the boy pouted. "Do I have to?"

Nat answered with respectful frankness. "The only thing you *have* to do in life is die. But please, do it as a favor to me." He set the remote aside and returned to intently twiddling on his palm-top, a TV in its own right.

Tad was unnerved by Nat making a death joke to a child, but he always hesitated to criticize his brother, for fear of a sharp retort.

"And please, as a favor to me"— Rekha lifted her son tenderly onto her lap—"take off that headpiece before you suffocate."

When she tactfully removed it, Tad noted how, in the few months since he'd last seen his nephew, the boy's face had changed, becoming more angular where it had been round, as a puppy's muzzle slowly lengthens. Still, he was a slight boy, with sad dark eyes, and, if it's possible, sad dark hair. He was palpably smaller than his younger cousin Hunter, and, again, Tad saw 25 percent of his own genes in this frustrated child.

"I hate being seen," Little Nat complained. "I hate having people see my face!" Compliant to his mother but resentful to be so, he rejected her by wandering over to examine Hunter's model Lego home, perhaps with an eye to purchase, leaving only Darth Vader's head in her care. She put it aside and remarked, "They are so eager to be bigger than somebody."

"He's grown up so fast!" Mom said approvingly, but then sighed. "I just pray I live to see him graduate from high school." Tad remembered Mom making the same sighing statement about himself years ago, backstage after a school play, and how it had scared him, or, anyway, made him shiver with the idea that he'd been sinfully preoccupied with the fun of the moment. Mom always sighed even after she laughed, as if to remind everyone she would be resuming her customary burden now.

Rekha played along. "One day it's diapers and crying, and before you know it, it's designer sneakers and slightly deeper-pitched crying."

"I wish we lived in outer space," Nat Junior said to his Dad, as if the grown-up might arrange it.

"We do live in outer space," Nat pointed out without looking up. "Right in the middle of it. The thickness of the atmosphere makes you forget it sometimes, but earth is as far away from Orion as it is from us. In fact, it's *exactly* as far."

The TV had been left alive, or at least on, and a syndicated rerun of a program featuring what were supposed to be America's funniest home videos was showing endless loops of brides falling in swimming pools, party guests spilling from collapsed platforms, "look at me" children's tumbles from swings. "Planet of the Oops!" declared a title card that then faded to a commercial. Bloodletting, and death itself, of course, were off-limits here. Dad and Mom watched with resignation, as if they'd surrendered the party to strangers.

"Are your videos ever on television, Rekha?" Tad asked, to cure the silence, remembering she filmed wildlife scenes.

"Not often," Rekha answered with no sign of resentment. "There's not much demand for America's most transcendentally beautiful videos." Her factual take on the ineffable always impressed Tad. "Speaking of transcending . . . How is your thesis progressing?" Whereas junior college dropout Bonny and success-minded Les and Dad showed no interest in Tad's activities, Rekha and Nat had run the academic gauntlet themselves, and she had the educated habit of conversing with company even if she hadn't chosen it.

"Oh, thanks, Rekha. It's coming along, slowly but confusingly."

"And does it have a point yet?" she said just as evenly, so Tad couldn't decide how much of a joke was intended. "Or is it still a Michelin guidebook to the nonexistent?"

"Well, I think my premise is that no matter how far-fetched we think our imaginations are, our fantasies still end up looking pretty much like what we already have. Heaven, Hell, the starship *Enterprise,* Mount Olympus, Asgard—they all look a lot like royal courts, or city hall." He cocked his head toward his dozing dad, though he couldn't tell if Rekha registered the reference. "Angels and devils are all humans. Even monsters are just us on a bad day—Frankenstein, Dracula, Lord Vader. Bilateral symmetry, eyes, shoulders. It's never strange enough."

"So, even in fantasy there is no escape?" Rekha announced, the doctor distilling the data.

"Exactly!" Tad said. He delighted in Rekha and thrilled when he could engage her imagination. "Well, the Blob is a step in the right direction, but really, it's just lava with a touch of an IQ. And some of the Hopi folklore is so weird, I can't follow it, but maybe to them it was logical. And your man Brahma, sitting in a lotus that's growing out of his own navel, that's pretty freethinking."

Rekha continued smiling but said nothing, which made Tad feel he'd made a misstep. He had pretended to be crass for comedy's sake, always a risky posture.

"Well, and the way Brahma, Shiva, and Vishnu take turns being one another, how Hindu gods have multiple identities, that's beyond me, which is good."

Rekha's smile tightened. "I assume the Holy Trinity also baffles you?"

She was teasing him, secretly, unlike the over-the-counter abuse Nat always dished out. Here was a woman who could work a veil. "I always assumed they stood for yesterday, today, and tomorrow. Starting, going, stopping," he stammered.

"Well, then, there you are!" she said, closing the case, and turned her attention to her skinny six-year-old, who was now scaling a bookshelf of color-coordinated simulated classics. "Careful, Nathaniel! Don't climb on that! You'll break it and/or yourself."

"Oh, let him climb," Big Nat countered, but faintly. Fathers want to see their sons climb high, as if the child were their inner child's kite, but mothers want them to live to adult-hood.

Nat closed his palm-top for the moment and now, just as impassively, watched the TV Little Nat had graciously allowed to live. He pressed the channel-advance button rhythmically, every three seconds, less like a man in search of entertainment than a security guard surveying the corridors.

Tad tried again. "You're surfing those channels like the Ghost of Christmas Present—you know, flying over the rooftops to peek in all the windows." Past the game shows where someone was winning and someone was losing, past the football games where one team was winning and another was losing, past the ashen old movies where everyone weeping and laughing was now long dead.

"The Ghost of Christmas Present has a better-trimmed beard."

"And are you going to trim yours? You *are* going corporate now." Nat had been fired from a number of academic posi-tions, mostly because he didn't care to handle the politics at his base-camp colleges, and he always automatically recited the truth to his supervisors without ever positioning it for a soft landing, which they took as insubordination.

"Yeah. From ivory tower to torture chamber." He sighed and turned off the television with the remote, imitating the electric *ping* it made, and then Little Nat. "*Ftoink!* I destroy you!" He continued looking at the darkness on the face of the TV deep. Rekha coughed, but Tad couldn't tell if it was by choice or not.

"Oh no!" Bonny involuntarily called from the dining room. "The canary's dead!"

This exciting real-life violence brought Hunter and Little Nat back into the company. No one spoke for a few seconds, but the case seemed clear. Dad's smoking in the small space had killed the canary. Weirdly, it made Tad briefly consider a coal miner's life. What sort of job would he have to resort to in order to survive now? Would blue-collar labor be necessary? Mining? He'd worked at a chemical plant for one summer, and the din and sulfurous air was hell to him, only with hillbillies instead of sophisticated demons for company.

"Well . . . one less mouth to feed," Bonny said in a strangely detached monotone, and covered the cage. "Should have left it in the country." After bankruptcy and a bewitched husband, pet loss was just a maraschino cherry on her misfortune. The boys, to Tad's surprise, didn't seem to mind.

"It was more Mom's bird than mine," Hunter said flatly. "Birds don't even like you or anything. If it was a dog, I'd cry."

"I barely *knew* that bird," Little Nat pointed out.

"Good thing we're staying in a hotel," Nat said.

"Let's have a cease-fire on the smoking, all right?" Bonny suggested with surprising delicacy. "It can't be good for the boys. Or just do it out on the steps, okay, Dad?" She carried the cage out of the room.

Dad, without quite acknowledging his culpability, wandered out to use the bathroom, mumbling, "My old man used to smoke all the way through dinner. Back then, it was supposed to be an *appetizer.* . . ."

"The heart attack *affected* him," Mom said, as if it were classified information.

"I know, and, I mean, I realize it's usually just you and him," Tad said to Mom. "But Dad seems completely oblivious of others now!"

"He never *struck* you, did he?" Mom reminded Tad. It was her stock, lame but valid defense. Her generation had seen spankings galore, not to mention the atom bomb. She had a kind of morbid optimism that consisted of imagining worse scenarios than the one you were in, like watching news footage of a plane crash and saying, "That could have been us!" or pointing out when Nat cracked his head that he could have fractured his skull. When speeding drivers passed their car, Mom always said, "In a hurry to get to the *graveyard!*"

"You're right," Tad agreed limply. His father had never hit Tad because he was never anywhere near him. Still, Tad remembered seeing his dad walk the halls of Waterville City Hall, snappily greeting everyone by nickname, if not king of the hill, then deputy king of the hill. As a very little boy—a social climber even in the sandbox—Tad told his playmates his father *was* the mayor, and only when he found out that lies are quickly exposed did he accept that his father was a perpetual sidekick. Still, Dad's corny jokes once seemed glamorously new to his ears, and on the exciting rare occasions when Dad told the bedtime stories, they were full of secret agents and movie stars, and Dad himself was the government official who gave Goldilocks five to ten for breaking and entering. Tad could remember times of seeming blood connection, Dad's strong hand holding down Tad's head as he gave him a monthly home haircut in the basement, stabilizing him earthward, like the clutch of a minister at baptism. And when he had found out it was Dad who brought the gifts, not Santa, how thrilled he had been, how much better that was. It made him love his parents more.

"And he gave you life," Mom added as a clincher. It reminded Tad of a joke Dad had played on him on the morning he was to move into his freshman dorm at Hale. He'd given Tad a letter, which turned out to be a mock bill for $180,000, Dad's comical calculation of rent, tuition, and board charges Tad had accrued as a child. Everyone laughed it up, especially since Hale had given Tad a generous scholarship, but he had hoped for a letter of paternal confidence like the ones WASP youths reported getting in their autobiographies. Still, Dad gave him life, and Christmas presents, and if he seldom praised, neither did he criticize.

"No, Ma. I love Dad. I just don't want you to be alone. . . ." Tad instantly regretted pitching any treatments for nightmares that Mom didn't yet have in development.

She smiled faintly and changed the subject. "You haven't eaten a thing, Tad," she said, acknowledging his slant reference to his love for her with one of her own. "Your appetite's all right, isn't it? You're not sick and not telling us?"

"I'm fine!" Tad said with restraint, though his inner Donald Duck was jabbering curses. "It's just, I'll probably be eating all day, and Bonny's sled o'goodies looks like you should photograph it, rather than eat it."

"It is pretty! Did you see? She did all of us as cookies!" Sure enough, despite, or perhaps in defiance of, her grief, Bonny had made a platter of gingerbread men that included minimal renderings of the family members. Tad's likeness had cherry red hair, but otherwise it was identical to the rest, with three buttons in lieu of clothes.

"That's funny!" Tad was intrigued. "But who's supposed to eat which one? Do you eat only yourself? There's an odd voodoo aspect to it. . . ." Bonny returned from wherever she'd taken the canary cage. Dad could be heard clattering around the bathroom. "Don't overanalyze it," she said. "I sprayed them with a fixative, so they're like ornaments. You don't eat them, unless you're, like, starving! See the red ribbon hooks? You can hang them!"

"Like crucifixes!" Tad observed.

"Must everything be perverse to you guys?" Bonny was straightforward at least. Les had always been middle-of-the-road in his joke telling, so meeting Nat and Tad had confused her at first.

"Wait a second!" Nat called from his corner, apparently not missing a trick. "We also *eat* Jesus, don't forget! Hang and then eat! Communion includes inherent cannibalism."

Bonny shook her head. She was tired by the rudderless free association her brothers-in-law brought to brunch. "These are just . . . souvenirs."

"I'm sorry, Bonny," Tad said, remembering she'd had a disastrous few months. "I'm impressed. This is all very imaginative and labor-intensive, and with all the . . . well, confusion you've had!" He touched her hand, surprising himself. She looked surprised back at him.

"I can hardly wait till Jesus brings all the presents!" Hunter said out of the blue. He had wandered past with a cookie, and typically confused Santa with God, and goods with goodness. Both supermen enjoy omniscience and (on Christmas Eve) ubiquity, and Santa's list and Saint Peter's are basically identical. Santa's more fun than Jesus, and Tad always wished Jesus were more like Buddha, who more resembles Santa than skinny-marink mirthless Christ. Santa's like a rich, careless father, though. If he's so full of love, why doesn't he ever spend any quality time with his kids? Showering them with presents, but never being around for the crises. He doesn't even show up; he just leaves the presents behind. Jesus isn't exactly a live-in lover, either, Baptist infatuation spirituals—to the effect that Jesus

Never Jilts—aside, God and Santa are both supposedly devoted, but both are generally unavailable.

"Let me go check on Les," Bonny said. "I heard him getting up."

"She's a strong woman," Mom announced when Bonny left.

"Yup," Tad answered, again confused by conflicting feelings. Bonny was certainly lovely and hardworking, and she sometimes reminded him of his college girlfriend Inger Persson, except Bonny was blond out of determination and Inger was born that way, and Inger was Swedish and hip. Her parents had acted in the sixties art-house psychodramas of Gunnar Sternland, uttering lines like "I feel nothing but contempt for your emptiness!"—which to collegiate Tad had seemed more complicated than parents were capable of being. Inger had routinely seen them nude in saunas and even in their films, whereas Tad's mom thought looking under automobiles was somehow dirty if you weren't a licensed mechanic. Tad had been so proud to sleep with this tall, gorgeous, articulate girl whose ultraliberalism inclined her to sleep with the underdog—in this case, Tad. He'd used her, he knew now, to be the envy of all his dorm mates. He was turned on by her beauty to others. She'd been his trophy as Bonny was Les's, she was his White House rather than his Blue Lagoon. That had been and was still Tad's fatal flaw, trying to ascend, trying to be taller, wanting to eat what the big boys eat. Looking at the abundant desserts Bonny had laid out, Tad remembered panicking as a child when he lay in bed and heard Les and Nat breaking open a forbidden bag of cookies in the kitchen below, which meant he wouldn't get any. He felt trapped by his place in the food chain. All his life, he'd been a guppy trying to ingratiate himself with the dolphins.

Little Nat and Hunter emerged from the bedroom quarreling. "Fraid not!"

"Fraid so!"

"Fraid not!"

"Fraid so!"

"Now what's this all about?" Mom asked.

Nat theorized, "In either case, it involves being afraid."

The slightly older Nat junior asserted, "You may be taller than me now, but you'll never be older than me!"

"I hope I live to see them both married!" Mom said over their heads. She clearly lived to see these kids. Descendant worship.

Les wandered in wearing a bathrobe, with Bonny close behind, a discreet attendant who wanted her patient to walk on his own but stood ready to check any unsteadiness. His hair, which had been shaved off at the hospital before the doctors figured out that his self-surgery was complete, had grown out into a crew-cut like the kind Tad's Avenue B hipster friends wore in lieu of military service. Stranger was Les's glassy but benign expression. Nat closed his palm-top, and Mom couldn't conceal her apprehension.

"Hello . . . every . . . *body,*" Les said carefully, puzzling over the last word as if just realizing how strange it is to greet others' bodies. His eyes, usually bright with plans, focused on a far horizon like a savant at Shangri-la, or else like the accident survivors found wandering away from auto wrecks. "Here you are!" he added with unexpected vigor, as if he'd looked under the bed and in the closet for them earlier. "I thought there would be floating, you know, strings of things." He looked toward the ceiling. "Things on strings."

"What?" Tad asked cautiously, but he assumed Les was referring to Bonny's customary intricate decorations. Hunter and Little Nat looked unsure of what to do, but they looked at the ceiling, as well.

"He looks good with the crew cut," Dad piped in, trying to spin damage control on brain damage. Dad had always idealized his army days, vocally regretting that none of his sons had opted for armed service, despite the fact that postwar Hawaii had not given Dad much opportunity for heroics.

"Yes!" Les seemed pleased to understand anything he heard. "The crew! Part of the crew!" A hush fell, like a crisp bedsheet over a fresh corpse. Les giggled, though, and went over to the fireplace. He indicated the many greeting cards on the mantel. "Nat, this is funny!" He had a bond with adjacent brother Nat that hadn't extended through and down to Tad. "Some are for my shooting me and some are for Christmas!" Among the aggressive red holiday cards were diffident pastel Cheer cards, distinct from Get Well cards, because getting well isn't always an option.

"Yeah, incongruous!" Nat answered, unwilling to talk down even to the handicapped. "*Poig*-nant, even." He vocalized the *g* as if to mock anyone who would actually find it so.

"We're going Christmas shopping later," Les announced with pleasure.

"Yes!" Bonny replied, encouraging him.

"There're lots of nice things at Poverty Barn," Les added.

"Oh, we'll definitely go to Poverty Barn," Bonny answered tautly, and turned to Mom and Dad. "It's a sort of aphasia. The doctor says it may pass with time."

"It may pass with time," Les repeated supportively but with no obvious understanding, like a husband aye-ayeing his wife while reading the newspaper at the breakfast table. "Hello!" He smiled at the boys and at Tad, though it wasn't clear if he knew who they were.

"You want to eat something, or not?" Bonny used the slightly arch voice she applied to Hunter.

Les grinned. "Mm! Want to!" He didn't seem much like a corporate dynamo as he and Bonny went to find suitably soft food on the buffet table. Rekha took this moment to lead the boys back to their play station in the bedroom.

Nat eyed Tad with brotherly shorthand and muttered, "Imagine my surprise to encounter a frictionless surface." Tad had put Vaseline on Nat's bedroom doorknob one April Fools'

Day, and, waiting for his curse words, had only heard an intentionally loud musing from the other side of the door: "Imagine my surprise to encounter a frictionless surface." Ever since
then, the family had used the phrase whenever a mystifying
inconvenience presented itself.

"Shades of Frank the Crank," Dad whispered, alluding
to his own impressively impoverished childhood, which was
full of colorful sufferers. Frank the Crank was the retarded
middle-aged son Dad's next-door neighbors kept at home,
who wandered through Waterville mildly reciting obscenities
and discarded shiny objects as his consolation prizes for surviving the Depression.

"At least Les isn't hyperventilating like he used to. . . ." Tad
felt like he was pulling the family on a sled on a long, snowless
sidewalk.

"Life's not all butter and birthday cake," Mom declared,
then, inevitably, sighed. She'd always said this at challenging
moments, which had maddened Tad as a child because it made
the listener imagine butter applied to birthday cake. That went
beyond fun into nauseating. "You know, the morning of his
accident, I was looking out the window—you know, up in
Waterville," she began to recite. Tad had heard her tell this
story several times already, by phone, but she seemed to need
to tell it, like a rosary. "And what should I see in the bird feeder
but a big black crow! A crow, in Waterville! It gave me a bad
feeling."

Tad had heard of similar omens from his grandmother,
whose fear of the supernatural made Mom seem as rational as
Rekha, and as he contemplated his mother's ever-whiter hair,
he was moved by how much like his grandmother she now
was. It was because of Mom's mother that Tad had first fallen
in love with the strata of imaginary beings. She had taught him
to distinguish the trooping fairies from the solitary ones, those
lovelies that were cast out of heaven and those lowlies simply

belched up by creation, those that changed shape and those that were simply invisible. Softly, patiently, presenting simple facts, she told him of their lairs and throne rooms. When schoolboy Tad asked her pointedly if she truly believed in all these species of goblin, pixie, and pookah, she said, "I don't, personally, but I can't help it if they're *there*."

"Oh, sure!" said disbeliever Nat. "So the banshee's doing mere injuries now? I guess what with vaccines and the lower speed limits, death is down, he's gotta moonlight."

Tad felt Mom needed some support. "Well . . . I remember Gramma saying she saw the image of Grampa the same day they got the, uh, telegram." His grandmother had always said of her late husband, "He wasn't the man I married," but she meant it literally, that "the Good Folk" had replaced him with an evil look-alike, a gray-haired changeling who then left her and died, while her real, faithful husband languished but lived in a bejeweled cavern in Avalon. She called them the Good Folk instead of the Bad Folk they were because if they were invisibly nearby and heard you, you'd be cursed. The fairies in that sense were like Communist Russia.

"Oh, dear . . ." Mom trembled, restraining herself from crying. "I mustn't . . ." Tad remembered his grandmother telling him that the tears the living shed for the dead are poured into heavy oaken buckets, and the dead must carry them around, so it's best not to weep for them. He'd later learned that belief went back to the famine, a draconian therapy for the grief-stricken. In his grandmother's girlhood Ireland, even fantasy couldn't keep misery out of the picture. So Mom had been taught to conceal her emotions out of fear of ectoplasmic reprisals.

"Now, wait a second. I think Les seems happier now than he ever has," Nat pointed out, making the good news sound brutal somehow. "He's peaceful, which he never was before."

"He may be in a darlin' mood, but he's unemployable,"

Dad responded. Dad was clearly pained at the sight of the one son whose accomplishments excited him, the one nonegg-head, gone gutless. *Conquer, conquer, conquer,* Tad reflected. That's what men respect, and that's why some of them assess homosexuality as a failure. They imagine it's surrender instead of conquest. If Dad only knew, Tad mused, how he, too, was trying to scale the Alps or quell truculent natives. The few men he'd bedded, he was trying to control, to appropriate them, as if their muscles became his property for the duration. His blinkered sexuality was just as aggressive in its way as any old oil well, skyscraper, replicating chain of stores, spermlike spi-raling football or atom bomb disseminating itself, fertilizing the earth with death.

"Maybe he could walk dogs for the busy," Nat said with the straight face that he knew irked Dad.

"Here we are!" Bonny sounded like she was guiding a child down a precarious balance beam as she led Les to a seat by the television, then handed him a plastic mug of orange juice.

Dad changed the TV channel to a football game and chat-tered to the blank Les about which teams were where in the standings, compulsive small talk, as uttered in hospital rooms. As a child, Tad had wondered why his father gloated when a Boston team won anything. After all, Dad didn't deserve any credit for what the little men on the TV accomplished.

"They all want that one thing," Les mused, presumably meaning the football. "Why don't they just get two? Each side will have one. All settled!"

Tad was intrigued by Les's newfound pacifism. There was a time when Les and Dad had cared a great deal about stand-ings—batting averages, yards gained, who were the power bro-kers, who was the quarterback, the honcho, the mayor, the senator. Dad had always been eager to be near the power, while being secretly stung by lacking it himself. Tad remembered how Dad always trailed after Mayor Halloran like the mad doctor's dwarf assistant, or, anyway, like the jester beside the king. Were Tad's desires as inherited as his height?

Tad wondered what would happen to Les. Cheer without Getting Well? And Bonny would have a hard time with her in-laws on her hands for another week. For a moment, his own problems were not on his mind. He also noticed that Les, despite his disorientation, was nonetheless still glisteningly clean-shaven. At the height of his empire, Les had been his own TV spokesman for the VitaManager stores, always presenting himself by saying, "I'm not only the owner—I'm my best customer!" His smooth Wonder Boy face always seemed headed for the camera like an approaching meteor or polished limousine, and in close-up, no one knew he was only five foot three.

"Les, you're clean-shaven!" Tad tried direct address, but Les seemed absorbed in a TV commercial about a drumbeating toy rabbit using batteries that never run out.

"Stop! Rabbit!" he joked, presumably aware the TV couldn't hear him, and turned to Dad. "Too much drums!"

"Yes indeed!" Bonny said, tapping his mug to remind him to drink.

"That's what's wrong with the world! Too much drums." Tad joked. "Does he shave himself?" He now reverted to case study.

"Not yet. I shave him," Bonny said. "Don't I, Les?"

He nodded. "I used to drive there myself."

"Every day?" Tad asked her.

"Every day. This way, I see the man I know. And my mother says if you keep groomed, you'll make it through." She stroked Les's head, and he smiled.

"That's nice," he said. "I want to be a dog."

Tad was confusingly impressed. What he had taken to be Bonny's hardness now had a kindlier connotation—steadfastness. She had always insisted on mown lawns and pictures hung at matching heights, but Tad supposed it was her way of staving off meaninglessness. A square does make more sense than a squiggle.

"Oh, Tad!" Bonny said. "This is as good a time as any for the cake. Can I have the birthday candles?"

Tad felt the shock he'd had whenever a teacher announced a spot quiz. "Bonny, I—forgot!" To his surprise, Bonny, whom he'd imagined as relentless as a bullet train, began to cry. She had survived the tornado, only to be pierced by a straw. Les looked confused but remained in his seat. Rekha came in from the bedroom.

"Goodness, Bonny, are you all right?" She went to Bonny and held her, a surprising gesture for two differently aloof women.

Bonny composed herself quickly. "I'm just tired. Thanks."

"You've been working too hard!" Rekha seemed to offer praise and criticism at once. They stood apart again, self-consciously, with Mom and Dad looking on.

"Oh my God, I've been distracted. I forgot!" Tad repeated. "I'll go get some candles right now!"

"You don't have to," Bonny said. "I wasn't crying about the candles."

"I know, but I want to go! I bet Les will actually enjoy them!"

"Well, that's true. All right, then!" Bonny went to the bathroom to splash some water on her face.

"I'll go with you," Nat said, to Tad's surprise, and stood.

Rekha's eyes widened subtly. "Well now, what shall we do in your possibly protracted absence?" She did a playful imitation of a colonial British accent, but Tad could tell she was asking not to be left to tend to drunken Dad and sunken Les.

Nat shrugged typically. "Hand out the presents. That'll make for some busy work."

Mom trotted out her crestfallen face. "Don't you want to be here to see everyone's expressions when they open their gifts?"

Nat joined Tad at the door. "Naah, I'll just study the results. Anyhow, Tad will need help carrying the birthday candles."

Tad tried to feel insulted, but in this case he actually enjoyed picturing Tom Thumb, struggling to fend off a mouse with a lit birthday candle. *Colossal Planet.*

At the door, he playfully grasped the doorknob and re-enacted their fraternal punch line, hoping again to reattach some connection to Nat. "Imagine my surprise to encounter a frictionless surface!"

"Skip the shtick. See you all shortly!"

"Be careful!" Mom called.

Outside, the two brothers felt the easier confidentiality siblings share when their parents aren't around. Even the frigid air was a bond.

"In a way, Les seems to be having a nice vacation," Tad offered.

"Mm. The permanent vacation as described by the old girl groups. I hope his insurance is intact. I'd offer to look into it, but I assume Bonny knows what she's doing."

A young couple passed them, hand in hand and walking a golden retriever. Tad assumed it was a new relationship. "It's Dad I'm worried about," he said. "It was fine when he was fifty, but he's seventy now."

"The old man's just lost it," Nat announced simply. "He wants out of consciousness, I'd guess. Barely noon and the snake is out." He was referring to the vein that bulged from Dad's temple when he drank. "Luckily, the kids don't seem to care. They don't mind Les all that much, either. Kids just adjust and proceed." Tad remembered being oddly tear-less after his grandmother's death, even though he'd loved her, and the odd sensation of how fun it was playing impromptu

touch football with a rolled-up coat in the funeral parlor basement with the other children who were bored by the wake
upstairs.

"So . . . Little Nat does like that Darth Vader costume I
sent him."

"Yeah yeah, Thanks, in quotes. The fact is, he hides in it.
I think he's just getting to the point where he's self-conscious
about how he looks."

"What, that he's small for his age?"

"Well, yeah, and that he's of mixed race. The kids in his
class are really aware of that stuff all of a sudden, and he doesn't
like being unique."

"But it'll be so cool eventually. He'll be so beautiful—"
Tad realized as he spoke this was not vocabulary Nat wanted to
hear about his son. "Er, or handsome. You know what I mean.
Anyway, the world he'll be an adult in will be more enlight-
ened than Dad's and Mom's was. "

"We hope. You can't tell a kid to wait ten years to be hip."

"And also, he'll have the advantage—what is it called in
biology? Heterosis. Hybrid vigor." Tad tried to show off any
science skills he could summon with Nat. It was his version of
keeping up with the Joneses.

The cold now put a wedge between them. "So, what did
you get Rekha?" Tad continued.

"Nothing. We don't exchange gifts. It's a waste of resources.
And it's our way of showing we trust each other." Nat had once
argued against cemeteries as a waste of resources in Debating
Club at Waterville Latin, to the censure of the priest moderat-
ing. Twelve-year-old Tad had thought that was extremely hip, as
if Nat were the Lucifer of logic.

"Oh, that's right, I forgot. But it's a gesture, isn't it, a love
refresher, a necessary ritual?"

"Ritual is just delusion made legal," Nat stated, as if re-
counting the major export of a foreign country. Tad thought

of the typed postcard he'd received in the mail ten years before, announcing Nat and Rekha's marriage like a change of address. When Nat and Rekha got serious, they didn't get romantic. They got serious. As a couple, they seemed to have a hermetically private relationship, a secret society like the Masons, or the Thuggees, or the Serpent Club at Hale. "By the way," Nat added, "what's with the tight leather and no hat? You're not a delinquent teenager. You're entering middle age." Nat wore an Arctic explorer-style bulky parka with a fur-lined hood. He had no problem with fur—if you can kill it, he figured, as a Darwinian, it had it coming.

Tad tentatively stood his ground. "It's not that tight."

"I just don't want you to embarrass yourself."

Tad tensed up again. What Nat meant was that he didn't want Tad to embarrass him. "Are you annoyed with me about something?"

Nat didn't answer at once. "Only that you ask annoying questions like whether I'm annoyed with you," he said sharply, but then took a reactive breath. "Hey, Les's body-snatcher routine is weirding me out, and pretending to be up, up, up for this job interview wore me out, and Dad is Dad, and if I can't take it out on my little brother, who can I?"

Somehow this seemed a friendly concession from Nat. "Well, I know . . ." Tad felt like this was a bargaining table with two tiny nations. "But what about Rekha—can't you be mad at, or with, her?"

Nat exhaled a one-note whistle. "Oh no. It doesn't work that way."

Tad knew Nat knew about Angelo, but it had never been acknowledged in words. "Are you annoyed with me for being gay?" he ventured. Both Nat and Tad had been schooled in the Waterville Latin assumption that gayness was a choice one made to get attention, though why anyone wanted the kind of attention it garnered was never fully explained.

"No, no," Nat answered hotly. "That's perfectly natural. Rekha and I knew some gay elephants in Bombay. They showed them heterosexual pachyderm porn, but it didn't change anything. There are alcoholic elephants, too. They seek out fermented fruit."

Tad didn't like the equation of gayness and alcoholism, but he curbed his objection because he longed for peace with his brother, and at the moment, he needed friendly counsel rather than a debate. "For some reason, lately, I'm not even sure I actually am gay."

Nat stopped in his tracks, the performer in him overplaying the gesture. He spread his arms wide. "Whoa! What am I holding here?"

Tad flinched, recognizing a private childhood joke, deployed to express disbelief. "World's largest invisible coffee cup," he murmured.

Nat now drum-rolled his lips like a fidgety horse. "And what is this I'm doing?" he recited.

Tad sighed. "World's largest spit take."

"Exactly. Taxonomy check! Eight legs makes an arachnid! If you're not gay, what about those five years you spent playing house with Pinocchio?" Despite his doctorate, Nat prided himself on his Waterville street-life frankness.

"Well, exactly, I think we were just playing house. I was the husband, I felt safe with him. But most men are disgusting, and self-absorbed! I admire women, but somehow I'm not ready."

Nat had to decide if he was going to walk through this mental mud puddle or not. "Well . . . laddie, you are more confused than an anal-retentive anarchist. You're thirty-four and think maybe you're still just afraid of girls?"

"Well, we are Irish. And . . . I mean, women are a better species. I like the way they've got this war and murder thing beat, for the most part."

"I like Isaac Newton, but that doesn't mean I want to sleep with him."

"Well, and, at least with men being with women, it's clear who's on top and who's on the bottom."

Nat stopped again, spreading his arms even wider this time. "What am I holding?" he repeated.

"Oh come on," Tad protested, but he played along to prevent a quarrel. "World's largest invisible coffee cup. . . ."

"No!" Nat said intensely. "Largest invisible coffee cup *in the universe*. Boyo, if you think the way men and women relate is as simple as that, you really are even more childish than I ever suspected."

This grieved Tad, the knowledge that however much fun they could share, however allied to provide color commentary on the world's widescreen burlesque, in his heart Nat saw Tad as junior varsity, second string, a noncompetitor in the arena. Nat's unspoken theory was that gay men could handle the solitary stuff—the weight lifting, the diving, the one-night stands—but straight men still excelled at boxing and marriage.

They walked in silence for a minute. "I just meant, you know, traditionally. . . . The way sky and earth are male and female in Greek mythology, because the sky is on top. . . ." Tad looked to Nat, but the session was over.

Somewhere, church bells rang, girlishly and gravely, and Tad remembered it was Sunday, and none of the Learys had even mentioned considering going to Mass. He'd stopped going his freshman week at Hale, but he thought Mom still went, as if to get credit from her own long-dead mother for taking her castor oil.

The corner deli was overheated and crowded with late-rising brunch shoppers, but still a relief from the gray cold outside. A hand-lettered cardboard sign on the cash register declared: "BEST" COFFEE IN TOWN. Tad liked the quotation marks around the word *best,* as if their coffee wasn't really the best, or else the whole idea of best was somehow debatable.

"Tony? I have a void!" A pretty teenaged Hispanic woman behind the counter was calling to the stockroom. Her large liquidy eyes made Tad think of Angelo. "I have a void! Can you help me fix that?" An impatient-looking old Caucasian codger stood by, drumming his fingers on his purple down jacket. The closeness of the shelves, the milling customers, oxenlike in their winter wear, and the excess heat felt to Tad—who compulsively converted *here* to *elsewhere* in his mind—as if he were in a tiny stable, a manger, whatever a manger is.

Over the counter hung a breakfast menu labeled BARN-YARD SUGGESTIONS, which struck Tad as slang for talking dirty. As decoration, a cartoon pig and chicken merrily offered the viewer a plate of bacon and eggs. Tad nudged Nat, hoping, as always, that the right joke would win his brother's respect.

"Look at that!" He pretended to gasp. "Do those animals have any idea what they're doing?"

Nat played along automatically. "I think therapy has taught them to embrace their destinies."

"Mm," Tad continued. "Deli Be My Destiny."

"It's like Dad serving up his liver on a platter," Nat went on. Before Tad could gasp, this time sincerely, Nat had calmly refocused his attention to the pretty salesclerk. "Do you carry birthday candles, like for cake?" he asked, carefully specific.

"Are the candles for Baby Jesus' birthday?" she asked playfully, her brown eyes like inviting ponds boys play hooky to swim in. Tad liked that. Her soft neck. The moment was jarred by the appearance of Tony, a large, dented version of handsome, who pressed a button, resolved her void, and valiantly retreated to the stockroom. Which one did Tad want?

Nat never flirted. "No, for a human," he said over the register's clicking.

The girl produced a tiny box of candles from somewhere behind the counter, and Nat quickly paid for them.

Tad was surprised. "Nat! It was my mistake. I should pay for them."

"Forget it," Nat said. "I'm pulling a mini-Jesus."

The young cashier smiled but knew not to intrude on New Yorkers' private conversations. She put the candles in a bag that read WE LOVE OUR CUSTOMERS. Instead of the word *love* was the happy, symmetrical symbol for the heart, so unlike the squishy, unbalanced actual organ. The girl looked radiantly at Tad as she gave Nat his change and said, "Happy birthday!"

"Yes, same to you!" Tad answered nonsensically, aroused but aware it was only his ego that was. Then it dawned on him that she had used that goo-goo inflection on him that is reserved for children. His possible love object thought he was younger than she was.

Suddenly, the edgy man in the down jacket started barking in agitation, something about how a customer who'd just left must have stolen his wallet. "I'll bet it's a racket, and you people are in on it!" he shouted to the frightened young woman. Tad considered chasing the suspect to impress Nat, but Tony, the cashier's void-fixer, had already sprinted out after someone he hadn't even seen, leaving the crowded store in silent confusion.

After a few seconds, the panicky man discovered his wallet in his jacket pocket. "Oh, wait—no, here it is!" He had to be loud to stop the tension ball he'd gotten rolling, but he clearly also tried to underplay it as an event. Tony returned out of breath and empty-handed, since there was no one to capture. Tad and Nat stared uncomfortably, and the accusing man observed, "I used to live in New York, but it's stuff like this that made me leave." His illogic reminded Tad of Justin's mother. So much unnecessary trouble. The old man had probably provoked that void, too, Tad concluded.

The odd experience made the return walk feel slightly out

of kilter. "So—you said you've been distracted?" Nat began. "What's distracting you?"

"Well . . ." Tad decided to confide in Nat, especially since Nat had asked. "Do not tell Mom or Dad this, with all they have to deal with. . . . My friend Garth is returning to New York next week and I have to find a new place to live." He left out the more distracting getting fired part, knowing Nat might somehow suspect Tad of being guilty as charged.

"Don't they have spare cots at that school you teach at?" Nat asked. "I slept at my lab for a while, years ago."

Tad ad-libbed. "Well, the Health Board doesn't allow anyone to live there. . . ."

"I see. . . . Well, Sheep's Crossing can be your hideout for a . . . an hour or two. . . ." Nat smiled, his generosity couched in the mockery that made him able to offer it. "We don't move until the Epiphany."

"Whoa, thanks, Nat. I just don't know what's happening yet."

"There's your epitaph," said Nat. "TAD LEARY—I JUST DON'T KNOW WHAT'S HAPPENING YET." To Tad's amazement, Nat put his parka'd arm around his brother's leathered shoulder and gave him a reassuring squeeze. "That's human consciousness for ya!"

Back at Les's, which now seemed overheated from food and running children, or only by comparison with the cold outside, Les sat on the couch as Bonny fed him a soft-boiled egg, spoonful by spoonful. Tad remembered with grief and pleasure how Mom used to spoon-feed soft-boiled eggs to him long after he could do it for himself. Tad had sensed she enjoyed doing it, and he'd felt guilty as a gigolo when Dad had groused that spoiling the boy that way would turn him into a sissy. Mom turned her gaze from Les to Tad mournfully.

Tad tried to comfort her. He owed her for the eggs gone by. "He is okay, Mom. And he will get better. Remember when Angelo's sister was in that car crash and got amnesia? She thought her brothers were spies trying to kill her. She eventually got her memory back."

"I hope so," Mom said, though her inflection was hopeless. Across the room, Hunter and Nat junior had finished assembling the Visible Horse, an instructional medical model with a skeleton and pastel-colored viscera held inside a transparent horse's body.

"We didn't open any presents but the children's," Rekha explained. "I won't be here, but still, we don't want Christmas itself to be anticlimactic."

"Les and Bonny gave me the Visible Horse!" Nat junior called, and without thanking him, he addressed Les. "Is it a boy horse or a girl horse?" Tad couldn't tell if little Nat understood Les's condition or just was unimpressed by it.

"Doesn't it say?" Nat asked. Nat junior, already an avid reader, scrutinized the box the toy came in, the way he always examined the inner lids of board games for the more obscure rules. Tad noticed it was made by a company called the Nature Factory.

Mom tried to get back to old-fashioned sexlessness. "It isn't either one. It's a ghost, after all." Tad found her Gramma-like comment bemusing, but he reflected that in most pictorial representations, ghosts did tend to fizzle out at the waist, and trailed off like smoke or a kite tail. Presumably, the dead can't have kids.

"It's not dead—it's just *visible,*" junior scientist Nat maintained. "They just didn't include genitals!"

Mom gave a strangled hiccup of surprise.

"Come on, let's sing 'Happy Birthday,' maybe a few carols!" Tad resorted to a Yule duty he didn't like himself, but Mom played piano, and this could put her in a pleasant, diversionary spotlight for a few minutes. "Bonny, is that piano in tune?"

"I don't know. I just got it because *Modern Shelter* said it gave a room grace and purpose."

"Carol call! All wassail on deck!" Tad called to the boys, but they had gone into the bedroom, from which unearthly explosions and screams began to emanate. They were now immersed in installing Hunter's gift games, DinoZombie and Space Stalker, and refused to come out. The Visible Horse was apparently already forgotten and outdated, the eohippus at the auto show.

"*Carols* is just a code word for dumb old songs!" Hunter RSVP'd finally.

"Okay, you don't know what you're missing!" Tad found himself saying. Adulthood has a magic and sense of play that children in their seriousness know nothing about.

The adults first sang "Happy Birthday," with Mom accompanying in her plodding but reassuring way, like a burro ride. Les good-naturedly sang along, although he seemed to think the words were "Half a birthday to you, half a birthday to you," and when they got to his name, he just hummed, the way playful diners in restaurants do when they sing along for the benefit of a stranger's arriving cake at a nearby table.

Then Mom tried Christmas carols. As she played, sweet, childlike, perplexed concentration in her eyes as she summoned up chords from her rusty repertoire on the cozily out-of-tune piano, Tad remembered the happier times they'd had singing songs. She'd helped him learn the scores for school musicals, and it was one of the few times she seemed to relax and delight in being herself. Now she seemed disappointed that her onetime alter ego had become a problematic adult, and was, technically, hell-bound. She could never approve of him as wholeheartedly as she had when he'd gotten a standing ovation as Peter Pan, although even then, to public-conscious Les and private-minded Nat, Tad's acting had seemed an uneasy combination of exhibitionism and embarrassment. Tad again recalled he hadn't done his gift shopping, and he decided he'd give Mom a framed photo of himself onstage as Puck, glamorously sinking in half-light, almost as a plea for her to take him back on the terms that preceded his coming out. Dad didn't see drama as a varsity sport, or at least was unimpressed by Puck, but Mom might yet be his friend again.

Nat suggested they sing the parody lyrics he and Tad always devised for the duller carols. "King Kong Marilyn Monroe, Tintin and Bella Abzug!" he called, more energized than he had been all day.

It was his revenge on "Ding dong merrily on high in heav'n the bells are ringing." He hated its starchy version of joy, the odious onomatopoeia of *ding dong,* and the fact that *heav'n* was supposed to be sung, arduously, as one syllable.

"King Kong Marilyn Monroe! Tintin and Bella Abzug! King Kong Sara Lee and I have all been sent to Sing Sing!"

To Tad's delight, Les sat up and sang all the parody words exactly right, and then grinned with satisfaction. The group fell silent, except Mom, who barreled on. She was concentrating on hitting the right notes.

"Les! Good for you!" Bonny said.

"Songs are easier than talking," Les explained. "They're already there."

"He remembers the words! That's great, isn't it?" Tad blurted. He had always assumed Les disdained the indoor comedy antics Nat and Tad resorted to for a social life. "He's in there all right! Try another one!"

Mom, who didn't approve of parody, lumbered on into "God Rest Ye Merry, Gentlemen," its lugubriousness the musical equivalent of one of her sighs. Tad and Nat sang a few lines obligingly, but confusion arose about the lyrics.

> "God rest ye merry, gentlemen, let nothing you dismay.
> Remember Christ our Savior was born on Christmas Day,
> To save us all from Satan's power—"

"No!" Mom stopped playing. "'Woe and sin.' It's 'To save us all from woe and sin.'"

"Hmm. Alternate versions." Tad remembered hearing both at different times.

"Oh, so 'Satan's power' is too scary for Christmas carols," Nat suggested. "'Woe and sin' is tiring, but, relatively, it's blander."

"I don't want to be singing Christmas carols with Satan right in them!" Mom sounded dazed. She did have some of her mother's apprehensions.

"Like you don't expect the *Alien* during *Holiday Inn,*" Nat offered.

"Where's Les?" Rekha asked.

Les had wandered away, having turned his attention to the gingerbread men. He was walking one of them across the buffet table as if shopping in a town square. "Doughnuts?" he seemed to speak on its behalf. "Oh no! Cake doesn't eat other cake!"

The moment for singing had clearly passed. After a pause, from the bedroom there arose such a clatter, Nat and Rekha went to see what was the matter. The boys were arguing about the rules of who kills whom in DinoZombie, since the competing monsters were technically already dead. Tad had been bombarded all summer with media and children alike reciting the slogan of the hit movie the CD-ROM was tied into: *"They're dead, but they're not extinct!"*

Despite the noise, Dad was dozing again at this point, which made him seem eerily helpless, extinct but not dead. Tad shuddered at his father's stillness, as if Dad were rehearsing something more. In the dining room, Bonny whispered gently to Les. Tad suggested in this time-out that he might leave soon, to get to his matinee.

"I know your friends have invited you for Christmas Eve," Mom said. Tad had resorted to imaginary friends to give himself an out if he found the prospect of Christmas with the family too much in his confused condition. "You go ahead. We understand."

"Well . . . it's a big reception," he said. "So it doesn't matter to them if I'm there or not, so maybe I will join you all again."

"Good. I mean, well, if you can. We really didn't get much chance to catch up."

"No, Mom, I know, what with Dad and Les . . ."

"And Nat moving to Iowa!" She considered moving away as partial credit toward tragedy.

"Well, Illinois, yes."

"I hope God takes time off my stay in purgatory for all this," Mom said tremulously. Nat could be heard click-clicking on his palm-top in the other room, even above the electrically evoked dinosaur caws.

"Oh, Mom." Tad hugged her. "I think we're already *in* purgatory."

Mom didn't address this possible heresy. "Anyway . . . Like I said . . . If you want to be with your friends, we'll understand."

"Thanks, Mom. We'll see. I'll try." It dawned on Tad with a mixture of guilt and happiness that he was Mom's extramarital affair that had never happened. He had been her devoted consolation in Dad's decline, and he had disappointed her. Then he thought of the New Year's Eves of his childhood, in the house that was now about to be sold, when the Learys would go out on the back porch at midnight and bang pots and pans together and yell. It was the only time he'd ever heard his mother raise her voice.

"I'm sorry about giving up the house," he added.

"Well, it's not like it burned down," Mom observed, ever prorating loss. "We had forty years in that house." Fast away the old year passes.

Bonny walked Tad out, and gave him a "let's talk" look in the hallway. For a heated moment, Tad feared she was about to ask him not to touch Hunter, but she said, "Tad . . . Nat just told me. . . . You have to leave your sublet."

"I didn't want to worry anyone, what with everything else. . . ."

"I understand. I just want you to know, if you really need someplace to stay, come stay on the couch here."

"Bonny, you're crowded here as it is! Mom and Dad must be driving you—" Tad felt dizzy, to find himself confiding in Bonny about his parents' failings.

"You could help me get through this. And Hunter's crazy about you, he is. He doesn't forget you, he just gets shy when he's not around you for a while."

Tad hadn't expected her goodness, and he shuddered at the depth he now saw existed where he'd only seen shallows. Nonetheless, that didn't mean he'd look forward to living on her couch and in her crisis.

"Oh, Bonny, that's so generous. But with all you've got to deal with . . ."

"Well, the doctors say Les might recover, not completely, but enough so he'd be like, well, nonexecutives. . . ." Tad wondered if she'd add "like you." What she said was, "Gardening, one doctor suggested."

Tad thought of Angelo's family, the Silvarinis, and their typically grating but ultimately truly named High-Class Gardeners business. "Plants don't talk," Mr. Silvarini had once told Tad, as one reason he liked his work. He seemed happy enough—after all, he leapt up at dawn at age seventy. Les might yet find a hitherto-unacceptable happiness.

"Yes, you said he might recover." Tad hurried back into the moment. "I hope so." He liked this lackadaisical Les more than the tightly wound self-whipping charioteer, leaping from phone to fax as if every minute were the final minute of a free shopping spree. "Anyway, let me see what happens. I'll call you tomorrow."

"Your mother really wants you to come back for Christmas Eve."

"I know." Tad squirmed. "I have plans, but . . . I probably will."

"It sounds like I shouldn't count on you to play Santa."

"I'm just confused, Bonny. Um . . . do you really need someone to play Santa?"

She laughed, to his surprise. "Oh, looking for a good role! No, the kids are too sophisticated for that. I just mean, it sounds like you don't want to come."

"I do, Bonny, I . . . You know, Les seems healthy, in a way."

"Yes. But children—and this child has a child of his own . . . can't survive without . . . sponsorship?" She squinted, as if she barely understood herself.

"Yes, I have no answer, or cure, for that. Well . . . Thanks so much, Bonny. I'll call you . . . tomorrow!" Tad said. He had found a friend in an unexpected relative.

"Your folks have only so many more times to see you!" Bonny reminded him as he walked away.

Tad was unnerved. Bonny, the supposed trophy, had made exactly the right point.

3. Revels with Rivals

Tad, aware he needed to conserve his spending now that he
was unemployed, decided to jam his hands in his pants pockets,
brave the cold, and walk down Second Avenue to get to the
East Village storefront where his next assembly was to be. At
more and more corners as he descended from workaday midtown to the residential Village, the medicinal smell of pine
boughs began to sting his nostrils like hot spice on the tongue
as he passed obtrusive displays of Christmas trees for sale. On
Manhattan's narrow sidewalks, the hulking tightly wrapped
trees loomed like moronic hair-netted goons in a police lineup.
After Christmas, Tad knew, they'd be seen discarded in doorways and curbsides like sleeping vagrants. He wondered who
the lumpen slouching salesmen were, in their long, incongruously silly striped elf hats, and what they did the rest of the
year, and whether this, too, was a job option he should consider, if he lived until the following Christmas. Again he
argued with himself, pointing out to himself he was sure to
live until next year, and for rent- and insurance-laden years to
come. He just had to wrassle reality on a more regular basis.

More relevantly, Tad wondered if any leads could be found for work or apartment at a struggling artist's version of a school play. Since breaking up with Angelo, Tad had failed to make close friends, and this crowd of overage undergrads was the closest to a circle he had located. Actor-landlord Garth was his connection to most of the expected guests, and Garth wouldn't be there. The prospect of performance art during the day disturbed him; at least midnight lent an aura of the magical to even the most mundane recitations about school-yard bullies and failed driving tests. Tad's friend by default would be appearing under his superantihero alias, or nom de kvetch, Orpheus 2000, but he was known to the collection agencies as Norman Mawk. Although he was a kind of mascot for his bohemian crowd—he was a threat to nobody—he had annoyed Tad at past parties, where he'd hijacked the proceedings to give little recitations, always announcing his solitude in joking ways that he thought were winsome—for example, through a bullhorn from a high window—but which Tad thought explained its perpetuation. He sympathized with Norman's highly self-publicized isolation but feared him as a chubby fun house-mirror reflection of his own worst self.

Tad walked past the dull upscale restaurants he had no interest in eating at, but he felt galled that he couldn't afford to. He passed the undistinguished-looking cross street that led to the United Nations, and down into the Twenties, where he paused at a thriving flower shop. Its outdoor racks bristled with pointy poinsettias and fashionably meager-looking wreaths made of twigs, which evoked uneasy memories of Christ's bleeding heart and crown of thorns on posters at Waterville Latin. Tad thought again of the loud, sloppy Silvarinis, who at first had seemed awful to his Hale-glazed eyes, when Angelo first trustingly brought him to a noisy Sunday dinner. The family lived in an always-rattling subdivision, where Waterville bordered both the Boston airport and the freeway, and were constantly shouting over the departing planes and passing cars, even when they were in good moods. The uncombed father and his three tank-topped sons comprised High-Class Gardeners—Angelo was the bookkeeper and occasional assistant—and although the business could not theoretically be high-class with a name like that, they still did beautiful work, especially on large indoor gardens in skyscrapers required by tax-break laws to include public spaces. They had looked like thugs, never read books, and drank wine out of Spider-Man tumblers, but they knew their roses, and Mr. Silvarini and his older sons always spoke of Angelo with a natural acceptance that surprised and pleased Tad, as an unexpected opposite family to his own. "It's how he always was," Terry, the eldest, had said, shrugging, one now-unplaceable summer morning in the Gordian past, continuing a now-forgotten conversation, popping open a breakfast beer can near some fragrant seedlings. Tad was visiting an outdoor site where all four Silvarini men were working, but he couldn't remember why. "His testicles didn't descend. It wasn't some *scheme* of his. It can't be a sin if it wasn't your decision."

The florist's piped-in, or, rather, piped-out, music blared an anonymous choir singing "Angels We Have Heard on High." Tad paused as he heard "and the mountains in reply, echoing their joyous strain . . ." Joyous strain? *Strain* meaning "melody" or *strain* meaning "difficulty"? *Joyous difficulty*—that was a good term for Tad's ambivalence about life. Now, watching the Korean florist and what Tad presumed were the man's sons loading a large tree into their delivery van, Tad missed Angelo's family.

Once in the Village, Tad headed east to Avenue B, past fire escape-obscured windows trimmed with snide young artists' intentionally insincere Christmas displays—dime-store reindeer with eyes as large as insect larvae, cutouts of elves with sexually ambiguous eyelashes—supposedly hostile but actually fond celebrations of their childhood rec rooms. Their campy cheerfulness was heightened by the trash cans and decrepit buildings, many of whose already shabby exteriors were painted black and decorated with skull or skeleton motifs whose gender, like Little Nat's gift horse, was also indeterminate. Tad thought of the Lugers, his family's lazy next-door neighbors in Waterville, who left their Christmas lights up all year but just didn't turn them on from January through November. Their swaybacked front porch always seemed on the verge of collapse, and twinkling lights festooning postponed disaster now brought them to mind.

Finally, he reached the bankrupt storefront whose windows had been covered with blankets to indicate renovation into a theater. Tad wondered if the evicted merchant was having a happy holiday. A cardboard poster in Magic Marker, looking like a student project at Excelsior, announced: "One perf only! Orpheus 2000." Underneath, in quotation marks, was the recommendation "A Tempest in a T-shirt!" but it was unattributed, so Tad assumed Norman was reviewing himself. In any case, he didn't want to go to anything called "a perf."

Norman's friend Yoni—her real, or anyway, legal name was unknown to Tad—was womanning the box office, in this case a card table just inside the door, with a cigar box full of singles. Yoni, an actress who had been part of the All-Nude Readers' Theater in the early seventies, was solid and graying now, her waist-length hair well shampooed but unconditioned, to suggest organic voluptuousness. She was listed in the classifieds as a "white witch and psychic masseuse" (she didn't actually touch her clients). She billed herself as a "hipstress" who, in addition to her hip duties, possessed "erotomantic" powers—you had to sleep with her to find out what they were—and, just as elusively, she claimed to have the power of invisibility, but only when no one else was around to not see her. Tad didn't know anyone she had massaged mentally, but she at least maintained high spirits and implicit independence, unlike the needy Norman.

"Tad! Here for the big show?" She smiled.

"No, Yoni, I'm here for Orpheus 2000!" he said, testy after his walk, his hands and ears numb.

"Now, now, peace on earth!" she chided. She wore a loose and much-patched peasant dress that seemed to make her peace's official calico watchdog.

"I know," Tad replied, trying to atone. "I just can't get over that stage name of his. Orpheus 2000! Why would he choose a futuristic name that is basically out-of-date already? It sounds like a computer from 1965. As cutting edge, it's got a short shelf life."

"Well, that's true," Yoni said, "but that's the beauty of Norman. He doesn't think things through like some *lawyer* would."

"Are you producing the show?" Tad asked, assuming that at this level the producer would also sell the tickets personally.

"No." Yoni grinned. "This isn't the kind of show that requires *producing*!" That didn't sound promising to Tad. "I said I'd work the box office if I could hand out flyers for *my* next performance! It's a Christmas Eve one-woman show, *The Virgin Mary's Tits.* The whole point is how the Virgin is just Ishtar and Rhea reworked, only with sexual denial added! I'm going to be serving cheese made from human breast milk! Isn't that truly Goddess?" Everyone in this crowd had a one-person show, and most of them were performing it sixteen hours a day. Presumably, they took nights off, since someone sleeping is an audience, not an actor.

Tad took one of Yoni's nearly illegible calligraphic handbills, imagining that the audience for such an event would be a virtual pantheon of the pathetic. He wondered whose milk would be used for the cheese, whether it was Yoni's or a specialty she'd ordered, but he didn't want to hear the details at that moment.

"It isn't really about Christmas, of course," Yoni explained. "It's Lupercalia and Saturnalia and Mithraism. Demeter and Persephone. The winter festival. The solstice. From screens to storm windows. Eat the harvest before it rots. You're in folklore, you *grok* this stuff!"

"I'm supposed to see my family that night," Tad murmured, and actually considered doing so. He thought again of the Silvarinis, who laughed lustily at dirty jokes but froze if the Virgin or Christ was spoken of with the least flippancy. Tad, still cocky from Hale, had told them what he thought was a harmless joke as their dinner guest, about a sulky teenaged Christ complaining, "I didn't ask to be born! My Dad just told me I would be!" Tad then had to pause uncomfortably, like a passenger at the border, as Angelo's parents argued in Italian and then held a silence for a moment before seeming normal again. The Silvarinis were obscene, but never profane.

"Well, it's free, in honor of Mithras, so bring them!" Yoni suggested. Tad forbade himself from imagining Mom at Yoni's topless sing-along sabbat. "Anyway . . . That'll be twenty dollars," Yoni added brightly.

"Twenty? On the phone, Norman told me it was ten. He also told me he'd commit suicide if I didn't come."

"Poor Norman. He has no head for business details!" Norman pretended to be helpless to get what he wanted all the time.

"Well, what's the charity? Stop the Gluttony?" Tad asked. Former binge-eater Yoni had organized a campaign to get "all you can eat" restaurants declared illegal on health grounds. *"You shouldn't eat all you can eat!"* The previous summer, she'd attempted to stop a hot dog-eating contest at Coney Island, only to be arrested and presented as a part of the comic proceedings on the local news. When she'd compared it to the unhealthiness of smoking, the contest coordinator pointed out that there's no such thing as secondhand fat.

"No. I'm not sure exactly what it benefits," Yoni admitted. "I think it's supposed to combat the slashing of NEA funding."

"Oh. I get it," Tad grumbled, and pulled a twenty from his wallet. "It's to benefit the USUNS." It was an infamous Leary family anecdote that, at the age of ten, future enterpreneur Les had carried around a can labeled "for the USUNS" while trick-or-treating on Halloween, and made a tidy haul, only to reveal afterward in a pretend hayseed's accent, as he pocketed the money, that the acronym stood for "us'ns."

"What's that?" Yoni looked puzzled.

"Nothing," Tad mumbled as she took the bill. He needed this rent party to find a new crib for himself. On the wall behind Yoni hung a rack of supposedly artistic, suspiciously free postcards, which on closer inspection proved to be advertisements for vodka and area restaurants and clothing shops. No matter how free of society's pretenses Yoni and Orpheus imagined themselves, they were still targeted consumers. Even a unicorn, presumably, must eat.

"Um . . . Yoni, Garth is coming back to town, and I need to find a new place to live. Do you know of any possibilities?"

"Not really. But . . . I'll keep my ears *open*." For some reason, Yoni made this sound as if it were a mystical yoga exercise. "Are you a cat person?"

"If need be," he said, picturing Yoni's friends' apartments, full of dried herbs and scented candles and pet cats that they imagined instructed them tacitly in the pagan ways.

"Anyway, mingle! Who knows? Enjoy the performance!"

"Does he shave his head onstage again?"

Yoni overacted innocence, as if she couldn't reveal the plot, and mimed zipping her mouth shut.

About sixty folding chairs had been set up, indicating the rear of the former store as the apparent playing area. Several dozen people were gathered, mostly underweight or overweight adults in the wrinkled casual wear of college students during exam period. Tad recognized some of their faces, but there was no one he could greet by name. He heard snippets of talk about grant applications and assistant directing, Web sites listing other Web sites, and cable TV shows that aired before dawn. At another card table like Yoni's were rice cakes and potato chips, offered right out of the bag, and white wine from a bag that was contained in a sort of cardboard keg. There was an open bag of Pecan Sandies, which Tad as a child had found so dry, he'd thought they were actually made of sand. In a limp acknowledgment of the season, there was also a bag of miniature candy canes, the cheapest and most rudimentary of holiday sweets, the one treat that is always left over.

Still, the refreshments were appropriate to the rec room feeling. With nothing else to do, Tad nervously poured himself a paper cup of the wine, which felt like milking a robot. It was at room temperature and he saw there was no ice. After sipping it to look busy, it occurred to him that he hadn't eaten anything at Les and Bonny's fine spread, and it was foolish to have passed up that buffet for this one. The wine was awful, as if intentionally, the way public housing is ugly as a reprimand to the poor. The East Village aesthetic in general, Tad thought, as he looked at the chipped black walls, seemed to equate dilapidation with truth.

He felt ground down by the subsistence-level wanness and useless ambition of this crowd, and the knowledge that even though his move from Boston had been three years ago, this was the closest he'd come to having a set. He'd relied on Angelo and the daily routine at Excelsior, and now, without them, he would go unwitnessed. At least in this group it was perfectly natural to be gay, but it didn't mean in his perpetual confusion he could find friendship any more natural.

"I didn't know white wine came in collapsible bags, like IV bags at the hospital!"

Tad turned around, to see Simon Kane, his nemesis in the Folklore Department at the Alternative College, who'd just manifested himself, clad in black, like a demon with the upper hand. Simon spoke a dozen languages, and Tad read everything in translation. Simon had published several critical essays, and Tad had never even written a Letter to the Editor. Simon was an expert on both ancient mythology and the Academy Awards, and was as obsessed with the latter's statistics (five times nominated but never a winner; the youngest winner in a nonacting category; the most nominations for one studio in a given year) as Tad's father was with baseball batting averages. Victory measured in decimal points.

Tad knew Simon had just gotten a reportedly fat book contract based on his still-unfinished doctoral thesis, which compared Mount Olympus's cast to Hollywood's, and Simon was grinning like a bad winner. He had the angular dark good looks of the sadistic nobleman whom the princess is contracted to marry, or the ham usually hired to play Satan, but his grin and his conversation were strained from an asphyxiating ambition to dazzle. Facts to him were weapons to stockpile. The force of his efforts frightened people who didn't want to spar with him at every moment. Like most damned souls, Simon primarily tormented himself.

"It's Tad the Paler!" He raised his plastic glass to Tad as if they were two civilized men about to meet on the field of honor for a duel. Simon's jokes were so doubly arcane that Tad had come to let them run over him without even trying to decipher them.

"Hi, Simon. I heard about your book deal! Congratulations!" Dog greet dog.

"Thank you! Whoever thought academia could pay off? Or my Oscar fetish, for that matter!" Tad wanted to look down on Simon's interests and ambitions, but he knew that, like most rivals, he and Simon were competing versions of the same person. When Tad had first slept with Inger, he remembered with discomfort, he'd been excited that she was the genetic offspring of an Academy Award nominee. "I told you that you should include Hollywood in that catalog of power structures you're doing."

Simon pretended not to grasp what Tad was writing about. "Well," Tad explained, "as fabulous as Hollywood is, it's not quite a fable. It does, in some ways, exist. I'm not interested in things that exist."

"That's your problem, isn't it?" Simon said in the friendly voice that is a technical excuse for unfriendliness. "You're not interested in things that exist." He then gazed around the room as if he hadn't heard himself speak, the way a child hurls a spitball and then looks elsewhere innocently. "Norman's little support group is out in force, I see," he commented, strategically changing the subject. Simon was one of the many people who didn't particularly like Norman but were somehow obliged to answer the roll call. "And what *provender!*" He arched his head toward the refreshments. "Poor Norman just can't grasp the quotidian details of hospitality!" Again, Norman seemed to have gotten a doctor's excuse from life. "So! . . ." Simon refocused his gaze on Tad. "How's your holiday? Are you getting SAD—you know, seasonal affected depression?"

"A little." Tad figured honesty would conceal his dislike.

"Ahh, so you're a *Noel Coward!*" Simon pushed his intelligence at you like it were a sable and you were the coat-check girl. He was always telling Tad what to read: *"What? You haven't read Botcht? You must! But don't bother unless you read him in the original High Middle German!"*

"Oh, there he is! Tad, this is my date, Gabe."

From the bobbing crowd, Simon produced, like a magician's trick, a small—though taller than Tad—blond man, who, Tad thought, seemed annoyed to be presented as Simon's date. "Gabe, this is Tad Leary. Tad's writing his thesis on the Bible and world mythology and just about everything else on earth, or, rather, everything that's not on earth, but with all due respect—" whenever Tad heard that phrase, he knew that whatever followed would be reliably respect-free "—he doesn't speak Hebrew or Greek or Norse, and his Latin couldn't get him work as an altar boy, even though he looks the part, so I don't know how he expects to know what he's talking about. His project will never be completed! It's as imaginary as its subject! He'll be a baby-sitter all his life!" His sudden success had made Simon giddy, and in his raptor's rapture he couldn't resist driving his shiny victory over his pedestrian cohorts. Tad shuddered at the possibility that Simon might find out about his dismissal from Excelsior and work that into his act.

"Well, my Klingon is pretty good," Tad returned, as if he hadn't taken offense, hoping his simple pop-culture reference showed him to be a regular guy, as opposed to Simon's relentless verbal Gatling gun. He was unexpectedly taken with Gabe, whose reddish face was pocked like a beautiful statue the neighbor kids have been firing BBs at. Gabe's brows were slightly knotted, as if he'd been staring right into the sun or contemplating an insoluble mental math problem for several years, but his blond eyelashes reminded Tad of long-lost Inger. Perhaps because Simon was his rival, Tad instantly coveted his date. However much Tad wished to want women, his wishes couldn't resist his desires. The brain is king, but the penis leads the rebels.

Simon started talking about his imminent trip to Los Angeles to study the Academy's archives and seek celluloid equivalents to Nereids, while Tad nodded and filched sidelong looks at Gabe. He responded simultaneously to the ageless man's beauty and, with relief, to his defects—the pockmarked red skin, the squint, the touch of gray, and the smoking, deducing from the pack of cigarettes in his shirt pocket. Altogether, it meant to Tad that—like currency whose value differs from one country to another—Gabe was nervous, imperfect enough that Tad might have a chance with him. He liked people to have problems; it kept them from being supercilious. Tad's condescending tenderness for Angelo's little frame had been deepened by Angelo's proportionally large appendix scar, which always reminded Tad of an animal rescued from a trap. Angelo would whimper and shiver when Tad eased onto him, like a dog still recovering from an earlier, cruel master. Tad had prided himself on being good to Angelo, but nonetheless the master.

"Oh, good for you," Gabe was saying to Simon, puzzled. He was a newcomer to this kind of patter.

"Is your full name Gabriel?" Tad asked, eager but at a loss. "You know, the messenger, the revealer, and the patron saint of radio?" He mimed playing a trumpet.

"No, just Gabe," the unwittingly contested prize returned. "My parents are former hippies. I think they thought giving me a farmer's name would make me organic or sincere or something." Tad thought of all the little Jebs and Zekes at Excelsior who went home to penthouses.

"And did it?" Simon asked lasciviously.

"Well, I'm studying to be a social worker. You do the case profile," Gabe answered simply. "You don't look old enough to be in college, but—what's your thesis about?" He turned to Tad, as if to take the sting out of Simon's comments and turn the conversation away from himself. Tad's preliminary judgment was that here was a thoughtful man, despite the inevitable frustrating allusion to Tad's immature face. He liked the exterior, so he was determined to approve the personality.

"It's about the hierarchies of imaginary places, gods, demigods, hemi-semi-demigods, bla bla bla . . ." Tad acted out self-deprecation, even though he meant it.

"Whoa, how can you study things that aren't there?"

"You know, like Simon said, mythology, literature, animated cartoons with hell in them, that kind of thing."

Gabe blinked. "So . . . the Bible is your only *factual* source?"

Tad was momentarily jarred. Either this man was devout, a delicious joker, or a mite stupid. Gabe saw Tad pause, and grinned. Bingo.

"And of all those tales, which do you believe?"

Tad chose to take Gabe's politeness as encouragement. "I don't believe anything, but I enjoy everything!" He beamed. "Jesus, Odin, Isis, Allah—they're rattlin' good stories!"

Simon didn't like this bonhomie, and he took Gabe's arm in a self-conscious "dinner is served" way. He led him to the chairs where their coats were folded. "Come on, Gabe, the so-called show is about to begin." Gabe gave Tad the same subtle eye roll in passing that the young nurse had given him on the subway. Conspiratorial, a possible ally.

Yoni had folded up the box office and now joined Tad. "Simon Cohen giving you attitude again?" she said sympathet-ically.

"Yoni, his name is *Kane*."

"No it isn't." She grinned, just a little wickedly for a sup-posed Earth Mother. "That Levantine panache? He's Jewish, and get this! He thinks it's a liability in his field!"

"In academia! Are you kidding? What about Einstein? Freud? How on earth can he imagine it's a liability?"

"Hey, why do supermodels think they're fat? Why don't billionaires ever think they have enough money? He thinks stardom is reserved for others, as if he himself just can't cut it. You must sometimes think being short and baby-faced is a lia-bility, when it isn't unless you let it be."

Yoni was right, but it irritated Tad to have her toss his fun-damental problem around like a Wiffle ball. The store's hang-ing lights began to darken, which seemed apt at the moment, and Tad and Yoni hurriedly took seats. As he removed his jacket, it occurred to Tad that Simon had once suggested that "Rumplestiltskin" was anti-Semitic, since it featured a dark stranger with a long name, who drove a hard bargain. Then he heard the groan of a heavy object being rolled onstage.

"Don't stand up during the performance," cautioned Yoni in a whisper. "They're videotaping it!"

When the lights came back up, they came up on the audience, too, because this was a storefront that didn't have specific light controls. Tad knew he'd be seen squirming on video if he squirmed, so even more stoicism would be required of him for the performance to come.

Norman, here theoretically transfigured as Orpheus 2000—though without his usual glitter-covered cardboard lyre and plastic laurel wreath—was reclining in a bathtub. It was on a pallet with casters, and that explained the pyramid builders' creaking Tad had just heard.

Please God, Tad thought, tell me he isn't going to be naked.

Norman's head was shaved, which was to be expected at this point, but Tad then noticed a weird design on Norman's face, and he realized in something like fright that Norman had gotten a tattoo of a goatee, a weird variation on Groucho's painted mustache. It combined the two fads Tad despised the most, because both despoiled the beauty of virgin skinland.

Please, God, he continued mentally. Tell me that's a drawing he can wash off.

"It's Christmas again!" Norman began with the ironic tone that constitutes the thick accent heard when hipsters speak English. He held up a battery-powered Santa toy, probably from the tourist-oriented outdoor toy bins of Chinatown, and pressed its on switch. Ear-piercing computer tones produced "Jingle Bells," technically accurate but as upsetting as a fire alarm. The electrified eyes of the toy Santa blazed bright green, like an evil space creature's disintegration gaze, and he was seated in a sports car rather than a sleigh.

Norman turned off the hellish toy and put it down with a sigh; presumably having proved his case against Christmas, he was now dismissing the witness. "Christ . . . Mess!" he recited, as if from a sacred text. "Christ . . . Missing! Christ . . . Mist!" Tad momentarily tried to comprehend what Norman was saying, but he quickly decided it would be better to let it all roll by inscrutably, like passing closed railroad cars blocking an auto's progress.

Norman stood up, as overweight as ever and—except for the promised T-shirt, which read LOST BOY—naked. Tad remembered Simon had nicknamed pale, thick Norman "The Abdominal Snowman." His flaccid penis nestled in his dry pubic hair like a fledgling in its nest, a badminton shuttlecock lost in a hedge. There was no water in the tub, evidently. What the tub had to do with anything, Tad couldn't figure, but again, he took himself to task for even trying to make sense of what he was seeing.

Norman allowed some time to pass before speaking again. "I'm . . . so . . . alone," he announced.

Tad bristled instinctively, his hands clutching his folding chair's seat as if he were encountering turbulence on a propeller plane. First of all, no man who shaves his head and has a tattoo of a goatee should talk about how lonely he is. Yes, Tad had sung "Where Is Love?" in *Oliver!* and enjoyed it, but he was thirteen years old at the time and theoretically playing someone else. However bad his problems were today, he wouldn't do anything like this. What mystified him was why Norman, who was five foot ten, chose to play the victim. He was a rhinoceros complaining about being slapped. Yes, it made Tad feel strong by comparison, but Norman's entire performance was yet to come, like a slog through a swamp of medical waste, and Tad would rather have paid the twenty dollars not to have to see it.

"People say they understand what it is to be alone, but they don't understand!" Orpheus went on, pacing the stage to provide action as well as dialogue. Only Norman—Tad agreed with himself wholeheartedly here—would have the innocent effrontery to get sixty friends to gather and give him twenty dollars each to listen to what was basically a midlife version of a child reciting "Itsy-Bitsy Spider," and then complain about how alone he was.

Onstage, Norman sipped a glass of actual wine, the usual signal of would-be avant-garde theater. Tad wondered if the monologue would be long enough to witness the wine's conversion to urine.

Norman—Tad just could not believe in the Orpheus character—continued. "I walk down the street and think, Look at all those happy couples! And even the people by themselves probably have someone waiting for them! I don't have anyone to comfort me when the threat of nuclear war frightens me!"

Nuclear war? Tad thought. He needs to get some fresh material. Since courtesy made him unable to move, Tad gazed at the painted-over water pipes overhead, seeking sensory alternatives to the monologue to come.

"I know you're expecting one of those 'How I Was Redeemed by a Child's Faith at Christmas' stories," Orpheus was saying. "But that just isn't going to happen."

Where do those pipes lead? Tad forced himself to wonder. To the East River, or a sewage-treatment plant in a distant borough? As a child, Tad had written notes to foreign children and flushed them down the toilet, hoping they'd be retrieved on an exotic shore and answered. In his already-bifurcated consciousness, he'd known enough not to put the notes in bottles, because that would clog the pipes, but he didn't quite face the fact that unprotected paper wasn't going to be legible, or even paper, by the time it emerged from its secret waterway.

Norman was continuing. "My family is from *Georgia*," he announced, as if the audience was to be impressed that he'd escaped. East Villagers were supposed to hoot at the South sight unseen as a deserving target of contempt, and, in fact, at family, as well. "My parents didn't accept me for who I was. I told them I wanted to go to acting school. Did they say, 'Whatever you want, precious, because we love you'? No. They said, 'Finish elementary school first!' When I told them I wanted to be a ballerina, did they support my dream? No.

They said I could be a ballet dancer but that I could *never* be a ballerina! I asked them for Oreos, and they brought home Hydrox instead! I wanted Hot Wheels for Christmas, and they got me some no-name toy cars from Japan! I asked for Malibu Stacy, and I got some no-name bimbo from the corner drug-store! They never took me to Disneyland! They never took me to Disney World! Neither the land nor the world! What did I get? Hilton Head! Six Flags Over Georgia! The State Fair!"

As he sometimes had during High Mass as a child, or whenever anything financial came up ever, Tad struggled to shut his ears and think about other things. He noticed the soft glow of the exit sign at the rear wall, and stared at the word EXIT. Would a reformed monster be called an Ex It?

"Well, *actually*," Norman went on, "they did take me to Disney World *finally*. But it was on the all-time record-breaking highest-attendance day *ever*. They kept announcing it over loudspeakers. My parents tried to act excited for my sake, like we were witnessing history, but I knew what it actually meant. Standing in long, long lines for rides I might not ever even get on!" Even amusement parks become Golgothas for those who wish them to be.

Time passed, Orpheus' anecdotes rose and fell. The words *gym teacher* and *recent surveys indicate* floated past. Like a prisoner of war resisting coercion to confess, Tad concentrated instead on the bowls of chips and stacks of transparent cups on the refreshment table, pretending they were a city on a distant world, not unlike the one he'd conjured from Dad's liquor cabinet. This outpost was a depot for food supplies for the surrounding galaxy. The box of wine was the tank where the rocket fuel was stored. The people of this planet were merce-naries, but at least they were undiscriminating in their tradings. Still, they were vulnerable to raids by pirates. No, Tad chastised himself. This fantasy is simply a credible variation on reality. Make this civilization more like unicellular flagellates or something unhuman.

Tad bobbed on a sea of drowsiness. Norman's performance continued to unspool. "Would the Antichrist have Antichristmas on June 25th?" Tad heard at one point. Norman certainly put the *snore* in *schnorrer*. Eventually, Tad resurfaced to scan the horizon. All he could tell was that Norman was discussing highlights of his own previous performances, and that somehow the NEA had tried to have Orpheus killed because he was classified as too beautiful to live.

"I am alone by the very nature of sociology and biology," Orpheus was saying. "And I think we should all file a class-action suit against both of them!"

Tad could sense this was nearing such climax as there would be.

"The world is indifferent to my simple request for fulfillment! There's no room at the inn! Happy Highly Hype-y Helly Holy Days! Geronimo!" Norman held up a razor blade, as if about to do a magic trick, and lightly and very quickly cut into his left wrist, then his right. Blackout.

The crowd obligingly gasped, though the aftershock was more confused than horrified. Tad, still irritated, mentally noted that Norman had, first of all, overlooked the fact that everyone in the audience had supported him, were in midsupport moment, in fact, and besides, he hadn't really cut deeply enough into his wrists to kill himself. Damned if he died, damned if he didn't.

Sure enough, the lights came up a few seconds later, with Norman in a bathrobe, bandages like puffy bracelets already containing whatever scratches he'd inflicted on himself.

Thank you! I love you! Norman mouthed without vocalizing, fantasizing that the perfunctory applause that greeted him was too thunderous for him to be heard over.

In the milling crowd afterward, Tad heard murmurs of commentary on Norman's performance.

"Well, he didn't die. So in that sense it was life-affirming."

"I liked it better when he played that little harp. It was funnier somehow."

"I enjoyed this more than that one he did where all we saw for an hour was an empty stage, while he was talking in the alley outside, because it was too personal for us to hear."

"Remember last year? When he pretended to be HIV-positive and he *wasn't*? It was supposed to be symbolic of loneliness or something, but anyway—he still hasn't worked up the nerve to tell his parents he's perfectly fine."

Tad downed another cup of the awful wine, hoping it would extinguish the smoke of irritation that would have been coming out of his ears in a comic strip. He couldn't see Gabe, but Yoni's welcoming face surfaced as the axis of the assembly turned. Simon was with her.

"Tad!" she called. "We were just talking! Norman's performance made us wonder. How would you like to die?"

Tad sighed. "Ohhhh . . . All right!"

"No, no." Yoni grinned, pushing him in mock chastisement. "I mean, if you had to die, how would you choose to? I'd take the traditional 'during orgasm' route."

"I'd be crushed by my admirers at my book signing," Simon mused.

"Saving someone's life?" Tad heard himself saying. "To make up for . . ."

"For what?" Simon asked suspiciously.

"I . . . don't know," Tad stuttered. "For the fact I probably never will save anyone's life?" He hadn't meant to answer honestly, but the presence of Simon always unbalanced him, especially since he supposed Simon was currently sleeping with the future he wanted.

Orpheus appeared in a robe, giggling and panting like a boxer after the fight. People complimented his performance, just as a school Christmas pageant usually is spared constructive criticism.

"Tad! I'm glad you made it! I hope you could identify!"

Tad didn't know how to field that hope. "Is the tattoo for this performance, or for all time?" he asked instead.

"No, it's just temporary! Like renting a car! I thought I'd see if it worked for me first." Tad, inexplicably, was relieved to hear this. He couldn't find words to speak in response, though.

"So . . ." Norman resumed. "Were you moved?"

"I was clutching my seat," Tad answered honestly. "You know . . . in your loneliness, you forgot to tell me the tickets were twenty dollars." He could be petty when necessary.

Orpheus groaned. "Between the rent for the theater and the guy I hired to videotape me, I'll be lucky if I break even." Here he was both the bride and the father of the bride simultaneously. "So, is there anyone here I can date?"

Again, Tad shuddered at Norman's offstage act—it seemed as much a performance as actual desire—but nonetheless, it reminded him of the pleasingly imperfect Gabe, and he scanned the room looking for him.

"Where's *your* alleged date?" he asked Simon.

"He stepped outside for a smoke," Simon said. "Nice, isn't he? Too bad he smokes."

Outside, Gabe was smoking like a temple candle under the canopy. Snow had begun to fall lightly but continuously, and it was sticking to the ground, making even this squalid street elegant. Tad decided that instead of a gaudy attempt at wit, a little black greeting would be best.

"The falling snow is beautiful, isn't it?"

"Yes," Gabe conceded. "But I don't want it to snow. It keeps me from getting around on my bicycle."

"I love to bicycle, too. It's like being a low-flying pedestrian." It was one of Tad's few ecstasies, coursing through chaos like a Jedi warrior past dangerous warships, whipping down the thundering narrow passage of parallel buses. He was the plucky sparrow at the buffalo stampede. Occasionally, truck drivers would shout "faggot" at him as they passed, but

Tad knew it wasn't personal. Hierarchically, all trucks regard bicycles as faggots.

"Mmmm." Gabe drew on his cigarette as if he were warming himself at a campfire. He hadn't put on his overcoat for this short outdoor break.

"You smoke, yet you bicycle everywhere?" Tad observed.

"Just your standard bundle of human contradictions."

"How long have you and Simon been dating?" Tad inquired with a studied casualness that nonetheless wobbled and landed heavily.

Gabe shuddered. "We aren't. This is a blind date. Well, a nearsighted date. I'd only seen him at a party I worked at with Yoni. She arranged for us to meet."

"He is dashing." Tad took the high road, and saluted himself for doing so.

"Yes, but he dashes too much! All that desperate show-off fact-firing! It's like he's auditioning to be the fastest pedant on earth. It's exhausting, like he's trying to *win* the conversation, and I don't see conversation as a contest!"

The snow appeared to be sticking to awnings and windowsills. "So why social work?" Tad ventured, knowing that expressing interest in the other is supposedly attractive.

"Just nosy, I guess," Gabe answered simply. "How did you get started in fantasy?"

"Well, in college I did a prank paper on inaccuracies in folklore—"

"You mean like the fact there are no ghosts, fairies, or witches?"

"No, not the magic. The inconsistencies. Like why all Cinderella's clothes, including one of the glass slippers, disappear at midnight, but not that one eternally solid shoe. And with the Three Bears—thermodynamically speaking, Baby Bear's bowl of porridge would have been the coldest, since it was the smallest, and would have lost heat the fastest."

"Ah! And I, well, as a kid I mean, always wondered how the giant could make bread from grinding the bones of Englishmen. Or how Peter Piper's peppers could be pickled before he even picked them."

"Oh, that's good! I hadn't thought of that!" This guy was great, but simultaneously Tad wondered if he was older or younger than himself. He was a little taller, but maybe that could work out.

"The food stuff always held my attention as a kid. On the last page of the picture book I was always looking at the banquet table, not the married couple." Gabe ground out his cigarette, which seemed like a bell ringing to mark the change of periods at school.

Tad tried to follow the current. "I'm headed back uptown. Are you free to walk with me?"

"I can't just dump Simon," Gabe said, pushing his cigarette stub off the sidewalk with his foot. "He paid for my ticket. I don't like him, but I don't want to mistreat him." Tad mentally told Diogenes to put down his lamp, because here was an honest man.

"Maybe we can get together another time?"

"Sure," Gabe said, though not as enthusiastically as Tad had hoped. "Yoni knows my number and probably my aura. But I have a job tonight. I'm in the FBI—Food and Beverage Industry. I cater for Triumphal Foods."

"What's your last name?"

"Pavlik."

"What is that, Polish?"

"Does it matter to you what nationality it is?"

"No, I . . . just want to get to know you better."

Gabe seemed abashed. "Sorry. New York dating has made me a little edgy."

Orpheus appeared in the doorway with an empty coffee can, still in his robe, asking for contributions one more time before the party ended. "Alms for the poor?" he thought he joked, and Tad winced at the tawdry Christmas with Baby Jane atmosphere. Darkness was already settling, along with the snow.

"I have to go," Tad told Norman.

"Oh, well, good-bye, then!" Gabe answered. Tad was now obliged to go, so he steered into the skid.

"Nice to meet you!" he called, but Gabe had headed inside. Norman gazed briefly at the falling snow. Tad noticed that despite the early hour, it was almost nightfall, the shortest day of the year. As a child attending movie matinees, Tad had found it disorienting to enter in sunlight and emerge in darkness.

"Eeuw!" Norman whined. "Snow! No wonder I didn't get as many people here as I'd hoped!"

"Oh, Norman, before I go . . ." Tad couldn't resist offering his suggestion. "Don't you want to start calling yourself Orpheus 3000 now, to stay cutting edge?"

"The problem with that is, 3000 doesn't even *sound* like a year," Norman frowned. "It's too strange on the ears. There will never be any year 3000."

Wow, Tad noted. Suicidal thoughts about time itself. "Well, happy New Year, while we still have them!"

He headed north, snowflakes momentarily clinging to his uncovered red hair as they would on a foraging fox. He was careful not to look back, as if, like Orpheus 2000 B.C., it might jinx his chances with his technically substanceless sweetheart in the netherworld.

4. Excelsior

Tad recklessly decided to take a cab uptown to peek masochistically at the Excelsior School's staff Christmas reception. He knew he shouldn't, but he told himself he wanted to gauge his fellow teachers' response to his getting fired. He imagined they might see him as a folk hero, via martyrdom, of Mr. Hyer's plutophilic rule. Most titillating of all, though, was the knowledge that he was excluded from the party, which made it mythical in its unavailability, even though it would be merely a minor adult version of recess. It made him ache to be there, just as knowing that Gabe was putatively Simon's inflamed his desire. At Hale, he'd despised the elitism of the mysterious Serpent Club but was hurt when they tapped his preppy dolt roommate and not him. At restaurants, the dinner special they'd just run out of always sounded most delicious to Tad.

"Cats have nine lives, but you don't!" cooed an actress's recorded voice in the cab. "So buckle up!" Something was wrong, though, and the tape played repeatedly as Tad rode uptown and passed the patchwork of store windows, brightening in contrast to the deepening darkness. "Cats have nine lives, but you don't! So buckle up! Cats have nine lives, but you don't! So buckle up!" Tad pleaded with the driver to turn it off, but the beleaguered African, who appeared to speak little English, indicated that the tape was broken and there was no choice but to endure the announcement until they reached their destination far up in the East Eighties. Signs scrolled past his window declaring BABY NEEDS GIFTS; GUARANTEED DELIVERY; EVERYTHING MUST GO. "Cats have nine lives, but you don't! So buckle up! Cats have nine lives, but you don't! So buckle up!" Tad began to worry that he was being warned against visiting the site of his humiliation.

Once he got out of the taxi, though, the falling snow and the stillness of the side street calmed him. He noticed through the window of the Italian restaurant indirectly across from Excelsior that its staff had all sat down to dinner together. Their black bow ties and white-aproned uniforms made them look all nearly identical, and their communion somehow reassured Tad. Despite the darkness, it was only five o'clock, too early for clangorous dinner crowds vying for seating. Wide avenues offer vistas, but narrow side streets offer epiphanies.

The school lay halfway between First and Second Avenue, and Tad was the only pedestrian in sight as he approached the converted town house. Here the snow was deeper, because fewer feet and auto tires had dissipated it. In the branches of the large curbside tree outside the school were several wind-blown plastic grocery bags, but what would ordinarily be an eyesore had been glorified by the snow, covered by it to resemble the nests of an unknown Arctic bird. Tad remembered seeing the school's custodian occasionally poking at previous such airborne litter with a rake, acting on Mr. Hyer's orders to keep a shipshape tree.

The lights were bright on the second story, and Tad knew the official party was up in the main activity room, with Mr. Hyer celebrating his first completed semester with trustees and otherwise-involved parents. He courted their company more than he did his staff's. There would be no children in the building, an odd sensation, compounded by the fact that Tad was going there at night and not during the day. It would be like visiting an amusement park when everything is locked and still.

He could see movement through the upper windows, but he didn't look directly at them, fearing the creepiness that would ensue if Justin's excitable mom or Mr. Hyer happened to look out and locked gazes with him, lurking there like a demented ragamuffin, ready to go postal despite the fact that this was a private school.

In the darker front bay window downstairs glowed two unrelated mechanical figures, secondhand electrified puppets from a department store's warehouse, donated by one of the students' chief-executive fathers. The scene didn't make much sense, since it consisted of an emphatically elderly elf hammering thin air—if he had ever had a toy to hammer, it was lost, but he neurotically persisted—and a robed Victorian choirboy, with a slowly lolling head and outspread arms, rotating in aimless benediction, or else in a lugubrious attempt at flight. The used choirboy's head had a wiring problem, however, and at the end of each of its rotations it would shiver as if from a nervous disorder. To Tad, it was the only moment when you might mistake the figure for alive.

In the unattended vestibule, warm but dank with wet boots and sodden overcoats, a student prankster had rearranged the letters on the bulletin board to say WELCOME SATAN. The party was a well-behaved one, and only a faint blur of conversing voices drifted down the banistered stairs. From the back of the ground floor, Tad heard more clearly the unguarded, liquor-loosened voice of one teacher he knew was also disgruntled, and he cautiously approached it. Now he knew why he'd risked awkward discovery. The sneaking around was exciting—it made him feel powerful.

He edged past the math and science room, which was unoccupied but had the lights on. On a blackboard full of calculations, someone had scrawled PLEASE SAVE, which intrigued Tad until he saw the next chalkboard, which read PLEASE DO NOT ERASE US!—a coy plea for their lives from normally emotionless numbers.

In the art room, off to the side, he heard several of the staff, who, presumably, were having a low-key but nonetheless imported beer, laughing. He could hear the gentle yet methodical voice of Irene, the music teacher.

"So we get to the part that goes 'Gone away is the blue bird, Here to stay is a new bird'—and Justin—he is so cute—asks me what the 'new bird' is exactly. And I say, 'I think it's a beautiful red cardinal!' And he says, 'But the cardinal is already here, it's not new!' I admit, I was stumped!"

Tad leaned through the doorway, as if presenting himself in parts would minimize any shock. "Well, I know it's just a ski-lodge ha-ha song, but any chance it could be the Holy Spirit?"

"Whoa! Tad!" said Margery, the math teacher. "What are *you* doing here?"

"I mean, we're glad to see you!" Irene amended, like that final fairy who takes the sting off the curse on Sleeping Beauty.

The two women were the only two people at this remote outpost of the festivities, but they were Tad's favorites on the teaching staff. Irene Weinstein and Margery Dawes had been confusing to Tad when he first joined the Excelsior staff. Irene was Chinese by birth and her adoptive parents, who rescued her from the "one child only and only boys matter" policy, were Jewish, and while Tad struggled to reconcile the text with the illustration, he also confused Irene's function with Margery's, who was black. Tad had presumed the Asian woman taught math and the black woman taught music, but it was exactly the opposite, and he could see the annoyance on

Margery's face when she kept having to correct his misconception. Further bewildering to him was the fact that she claimed never to have heard the nursery rhyme about "See-saw, Margery Daw, Jack shall have a new master." When she playfully accused him of making it up, he asked around for corroboration, but Irene, Mr. Hyer, foreigner Mimi, and the few children he recited it for all claimed never to have heard it in their lives. Tad kept meaning to find it in an anthology and show it to Margery, but adult duties kept distracting him from this trivia project.

"We just heard about what happened," Irene said, her voice keen, although she seemed unsure what to say. "I'm so sorry!"

"I'm angry," said Margery.

It was a typical response for both of them. Irene was sorry even when things weren't her fault, a weakness Tad found attractive. Margery got righteous regularly, which Tad admired but didn't find attractive, since he preferred relationships with the uncritical. There was something about being a fact-facer professionally, as with scientist Nat, that made sweetness unthinkable for Margery.

The room was being used to store supplies for the party upstairs, so pillars of unopened plastic cups and cartons of mixers surrounded them, giving the illusion these women were stevedores in nice dresses, taking a lazy work break. An opened box of chocolates sitting on a nearby table looked decimated. On the wall behind them were posted scrawled crayon pictures of Christmas trees that variously resembled maladjusted triangles, shaky electrical towers, shaggy rocket ships, or, inevitably, penises of other worlds. A manufactured poster on the side wall featured an intentionally clumsy sunflower drawn by an adult professional to resemble children's art, with the motto "Today is the first day of the rest of your life." Tad wanted to believe it, but it was a phrase that had become equated with self-delusory good cheer. He was more afraid that today might simply be the next day of his life so far.

"Honestly, I didn't do anything." Tad hoped to vindicate himself.

"Of course not! You don't have to defend yourself!" Margery assured him. "That woman is crazy, I think. Yip yip yip! It's like she's her own little nervous bites-everybody lap-dog!"

"What if Mr. Hyer catches you here?" Again, Irene's voice was concerned, but she had no idea what the consequences might be.

"Oh, relax," Margery, who was a beer ahead of Irene, countered. "I doubt he'll come down here, and even if he does, what can he do? He'll ask you to leave quietly. Andy's got his faults, but he's not gonna throw things." Margery referred to Mr. Hyer as Andy because his closely guarded first name was Andrew and she figured he'd detest being called Andy. "Have a beer with us."

"We're having our own little antiprom," Irene whispered, like the high school girl she still seemed to be. "The atmosphere upstairs was too stifling!"

"Yeah," said Margery. "Like I need to stand around and hear about proper Ritalin dosages from Rita." Rita was Justin's mother. Margery called people she didn't like by their first names, as a kind of stealthy disrespect. "Or about how her mailman has been withholding letters from her ex-husband! Truly! She is out of her mind!"

"Yeah, well, too bad she isn't out of her money," Tad sighed, then sat in a child's chair only slightly too small for him. "Then she might not have so much influence."

Margery, playing the bursar, handed Tad a bottle of beer from the case being stored nearby. Obviously, the crowd upstairs had shown no demand for beer. "And sugar, I'd rather live through last year's head lice-scare again than have another goal-structuring chat with Andy boy!"

As he began to twist the bottle cap off, Tad had a moment of self-doubt that it might require an opener and that he'd shred his flesh trying to remove it manually. Or, worse, that he'd be unable to open it even though it had a twist-off cap. Luckily, it yielded without incident. The beer was warm, but in a classroom it seemed enticingly out of place.

"I got some thank-you candy." Irene hesitantly indicated the nearly empty box.

"I'm afraid it's all over but the marzipan," Margery drawled.

"This is fine." Tad raised his bottle like a Eucharistic chalice.

"Honestly, Tad, it's outrageous, and I know once everyone comes back from Christmas break, they'll rally to get your job back," Irene said. "No one believes Rita."

Margery nodded, seconding the motion. "The woman's obtuse. Acutely obtuse, if that's geometrically possible."

Tad felt a rush of warmth like the ones he'd felt with Nat and Bonny earlier, when they'd offered their support unexpectedly. He tried to downplay it, in his nervous pride. "Thanks. We'll just have to wait and see. Um . . . what were you laughing about when I came in?"

Margery seemed to welcome changing the subject to round-edged mundanities. "We were just reviewing the chills and spills of the big Christmas performance."

"Oh, right!" Roiling in the flames of the newly fired, Tad had forgotten the school's Christmas program had been on Friday night. Irene could rule the eighty-eight keys of the piano like a tyrant, but she had trouble controlling her animate charges, lisping kindergartners meandering without concentration through what sounded like "Wise Up Shepherd and Holler." The devious boy who'd started the insincere "I love you" craze the previous month had conspiratorially enlisted all the older boys to change the words when they performed "On December Five and Twenty" to "Send My Gift in Fives and Twenties." It reminded Tad of his own juvenile song sabotage with Nat, and he wished he'd said good-bye to him at brunch.

"Personally, I thought it was funny," said realist Margery. "That song gave me the creeps. Did I hear those words right? 'To Mary born alive this cold December twenty-five.' Right there in A minor or whatever it is you have to think about the idea of a stillborn, outside, in subzero conditions! Whew! I've seen enough of that on the news!"

"Uh-oh!" Irene sat up. She heard footsteps and reacted like a teen caught passing notes. She had the talent to be a concert performer, but, like Tad, she got frightened at the miniature Judgment Day of auditions.

It was Mimi Milieu, the complacently unhelpful secretary who'd always screwed up Tad's projects without any hint of apology afterward. She had come down from the official party to fetch more paper napkins, and she wore the same pearls and perfectly tailored black suit that she wore every day. At first, she mistook Tad for a visiting student.

"Hello, *cheri*!" she grinned at him, odd behavior, considering she had sat beside Mr. Hyer as he fired Tad. As always, she then seemed startled to realize to whom she was speaking. "Oh! It's you!" Her mouth puckered as if from an unexpectedly sour drink. "I don't think you should be here!" She was the henchmadame, a svelte Smee to Mr. Hyer's Captain Hook, a flighty crocodile bird nervously removing the ticks that beset its vaster master.

Tad bluffed. "I came back to get my tools from my locker."

"What tools? You tell stories, you don't have any tools." Mimi didn't know he also didn't have a locker.

"I . . . Well, I just didn't get to say good-bye to anyone."

Mimi relented. Christmas tempered even her policy of intransigence. "But I tell you, you must not stay. I give you a five-minute warning. We do not want a scene."

Margery looked at the ceiling as if the proceedings were too embarrassing to watch. "You gonna summon the *gendarmes*?"

Mimi offered no comeback but the cold stare that is meant to indicate nobility that will not stoop. After she left the room, Irene took a relieved breath.

Margery returned her gaze to Tad. "I really can't bear that glorified receptionist Mimi! Mimi! Her name is so perfect. All she thinks about is Her Her!" For a moment, Tad in his Irishness felt like the ethnic three were in the servants' quarters, gossiping about the masters upstairs. At one time, this town house no doubt had had servants and masters.

"Hullo!"

It was Gordon, Irene's violinist boyfriend. He was mild and scrawny, with nineteenth-century-style wire-rim glasses and a ragged long coat. He had the unruly uncombed hair that gave classical music the nickname "longhair." Tad had noted there was a strain of straight man who could easily be mistaken for gay, who date Asian women. As always, though, bedroom politics are a secret society.

"Hi, Gordon!" Tad said, and stood. He had to go, and besides, he imagined Gordon's arrival introduced involuntary male rivalry he didn't want to conduct. Gordon was neutral and benign, but he was taller than Tad. He had also just been accepted by the Philharmonic, although he was to begin as the last-chair violin, so he was to be both exalted and demeaned simultaneously. Tad mentally filed a note that orchestras are hierarchies, too, with the violinist concertmaster as the conductor king's mistress or favorite son, and the semicircle fanned out from that center like a family tree. The percussion section haunted its periphery, the elegant violinists' caveman cousins, pounding the drums.

"Hi, Tad," Gordon returned, moderato. Either he hadn't heard about Tad's firing or it didn't affect him. Gordon hung his frayed old coat on the back of a chair, but it still spread out on the surrounding floor.

Mr. Hyer's booming, practiced laugh could be heard from upstairs. Tad assumed one of the trustees had just told an unfunny joke. "I'd better get going," he said, zipping up the jacket he'd never even taken off.

Irene took his hand, as if to pledge Tad for her sorority. "We know you didn't do anything wrong. He can't fire you for no reason."

"Well, it is a private school. We're not union employees or anything."

Margery offered a footnote. "Well, he is technically a member of the human race."

"Tad, we won't let it pass. You can count on us," Irene repeated.

Margery called after him as he left the room. "And even if worse comes to worst, you can make more money waiting tables than you do here."

"Well, I appreciate the support!" Tad called back. It was easier for him than being grateful eye-to-eye.

"Um . . . did I miss something?" he heard Gordon say.

Tad managed to slip out without encountering Mr. Hyer, so he considered his exploit as an espionage mission accomplished. He was ultimately headed to the West Village for dinner, so he walked west as far as Park Avenue, then downtown. The snow enrobed the street's intentional expense in intentionless simplicity. Tad passed glass and gold doorways of insincerely grinning doormen. He was glad there was no staff at Garth's building, so at least he owed no Christmas tips.

Snow was still falling. Somewhere, again, church bells began to ring, indicating six o'clock. Tad thought of the Angelus, and the workers he was descended from praying in the fields, of his grandmother saying the rosary to keep goblins at bay, and how she cautioned him not to walk the wrong way around a church, to the left, or widdershins, or he'd be liable to the penalty of permanent abduction to Avalon. That was part of her theory about what had happened to her arguably missing husband.

Tad impulsively decided to grab a cab again, to go downtown for what his college friend Minus had promised would be a small, peaceful dinner. Two cabs in one day was an almost-unprecedented expense for him, especially since he was unemployed now, but it excited him to be momentarily heedless, and he looked forward to this gathering. As the stores of all sorts and crowds of all stripes and looming clownish skyscrapers wheeled past again, made into phantasmic swirls by the darkness and the cab's speed, it occurred to him, organizer of universes that he was supposed to be, that the world was a beautiful full-color encyclopedia, only the entries were in random order and it was written in an indecipherable language.

5. God Bless Our Fame

Tad looked forward to seeing Minus Persson, who'd been overseas for years, but he was anxious about the possibility that Minus's sister, Inger, might be there, too, even though it was sixteen years since their strained affair. After its dissolution, he'd then found friendship with her brother, who was two years older and had lived off campus, in nonhermetic reality, away from the fumbling artificial hothouse of freshman social life. The two men had become close as Tad and Inger had drifted apart, like the Alpine man and lady who trade places on the old-fashioned cuckoo-clockish barometers. By Tad's senior year, when Tad was fed up with his rowdy, intolerant roomie, he and Minus had even shared an apartment in a part of Waterville that was actually worse than the one Tad grew up in.

Tad had developed a crush on Minus, who was skinny but straight, and who had laughed it off with a sophistication that impressed nineteen-year-old Tad. Since Minus was a progressive like his sister—he was named after the sensitive son in one of his parents' more pastoral movies—he even helped Tad assimilate the homosexuality Tad had hidden from himself in Waterville and from his roommate at Hale. They'd even briefly attempted to become a musical team, singing anachronistic folk oddities and acting out sophomoric sketches in basement coffeehouses that survived on open-mike nights. Long, lean Minus and pint-sized Tad made a funny contrasting visual, but their voices blended evenly when they sang their barbershop duets.

After the cab managed the intervening congestion of midtown, the choppy high seas between safe harbors, the West Village had a hushed domesticity that was similar to the Upper East Side, and there were no footprints at all in the deepening snow, Tad noticed as he emerged on Greenwich Street.

Minus and his wife and daughter had just moved back to New York, and Tad hadn't seen the town house they'd just moved into. The building was of old brick, with a short flight of stone steps and a reliable-looking forest green front door. As he worked the satisfying old brass knocker, Tad could see a fireplace through the window, its small blaze soundless through the glass. As the door opened, the reassuring sound and smell of limited, strictly controlled burning wood leapt out ahead of its master.

There was Minus, the unseated bygone object of his worship, five years older than the last time Tad had seen him, at the memorial service for his freshman roommate, who'd accidentally overdosed. He greeted Tad as if addressing Puck, knowing it was Tad's big role. "Are you 'that shrewd and knavish sprite called Robin Goodfellow'?"

Tad happily responded, luxuriating in the reference, "Aha! 'Thou speakest aright! I am that merry wanderer of the night.'"

Minus was bony and gregarious, with a horsey face, no conventional beauty like his younger sister, but his zest for the company of others and his energetic manner, as if he were always manning a sailboat in a bracing wind, had excited cannibal Tad in the same way Inger's plushness also had. Minus was balding now, and resembled the kindly, frizzy folktale farmer who rescues the abandoned baby. It was a kind of relief for Tad, since it mitigated his desire to make love to or replace or usurp him. To Tad, Minus was an idealized imperfect human.

"Tad, old tot! Good to see you!" His English had a slight British sound as well as a Swedish cast, because he'd learned it in Europe. "Ruth, I've known Tad since we were both little tiny unicellular organisms!" He led the old tot into the small living room, and over by the fire, which itself seemed Shakespearean. "Tad, this is my wife, Ruth."

Minus had married the daughter of the famous rotund slapstick movie comic Bobsy Baum, best remembered for his audible gulp and trademark catchphrase—like a bad child facing complications—"Ooo, what I did!" The couple had met in the mutual mixed backwash of her then newly late father's entourage and his own living father's at the Edinburgh Film Festival, where Bobsy was receiving a special after-the-fact lifetime achievement award. The famous rely on the fellow famous to overlook their fame, or, rather, look through it, like X-ray vision.

Ruth was unexpectedly stylish for the offspring of a baggy-pants loudmouth. She had short dark hair, the efficient "Mommy as Olympic event" cut, and wore a contrastingly demure black velvet dress with lace at the sleeves and collar. She was visibly pregnant, which reminded Tad of the Christmas cornucopia, filled to overflowing. "Nice to meet you, Tad!" She took his hand. If his height and baby face surprised her, she smoothly showed no evidence that it did. "This is like a highly distilled high school reunion, where I meet the friends from my husband's life before me!" Tad hadn't had the money to fly to Stockholm for their wedding. Her parents were both dead, so Minus's family locale had won.

"Yes! And may I be the last to congratulate you?" Tad nodded in her direction. "And on your incipient new daughter, too! Minus told me on the phone! That's great!"

"We're shooting for Groundhog Day, so she can come out and see her shadow!" Ruth showed unusual irreverence for an expectant mother. Tad could see in her face the wryness of her Jewish father, as well as the restraint of her beauty-contestant mother, a second-tier ingenue decades younger than Bobsy who gave famously wooden performances in Bobsy vehicles with names like *Destination Darling* or *Meet Sam Handwich*. Ruth had the seasoned poise of someone who'd been a child at parties full of famous adults, all of whom had bantered with her as a novelty alternative to chatting with their exes and rivals.

"This place is beautiful!" Tad felt at home, or at least in a good place. The fire reminded him of his junior suite at Hale, the only time he'd ever had a working fireplace. It had felt like borrowed comfort to him then, the pauper in the prince's chambers.

"Thanks! Or rather, thank Ruth! I was in England all fall, so I hadn't seen it myself till last week!" Minus had spent the last semester at Oxford, lackadaisically auditing a seminar on the films of Gunnar Sternland, whose alter ego his own father had often portrayed. Even Oxford was surrendering to the rule of pop culture, though Sternland's were as dire and unpop as movies got. Otherwise, Minus had spent his years sailing, playing tennis, traveling, and playing his guitar. He was one of the few whom the easy life actually relaxed. "We had to get a place in town. Ruth has to be here for—"

Ruth seemed eager to downplay whatever Minus was about to say. "It's a long, long story," she said, modestly but mysteriously. Tad sensed it was something bad.

Minus took Tad's jacket. "I see you're in your trademark jeans and white shirt! It's as if you're a character in a comic strip, always wearing exactly the same outfit!"

"My whole hope was that it would be noneccentric!" Tad explained.

"Ah yes, the wish to be mistaken for normal! I say, embrace your eccentricity!" Minus's voice had deepened in recent years, and Tad could hear his actor father's timbre in it now. "Our older daughter, already in progress, will be here in a minute. She's five, and she is *determined* to help wrap the presents for her grandparents!" Minus mimed Laocoön struggling with serpents. "It'll be just a small group, six or seven of us."

Tad noticed that Ruth was wearing a small silver pin on her chest, a female angel holding a swaddled infant.

"I like your pin!" he said, hoping a compliment would lubricate their alliance.

"Yes, you're the expert, I hear!" She smiled. "My mother gave it to me."

"I think it's Gabriel." Tad appraised the jewelry for meaning. "Silver's his color, too."

"His?" Ruth paused.

"Well, officially angels are male, but there's a tradition that in some circumstances, Gabriel *might* be a woman, and so protects expectant mothers."

"An Audubon of the ether!" Minus declared.

"Have you picked a name for the baby yet?" Tad asked.

"Ruth let me pick last time, so it's her turn." Minus smiled. Their partnership seemed steady.

She smiled almost imperceptibly. To Tad, men were dormant volcanoes, but women were still lakes teeming with secret life. "My grandmother's name was Esther, but I don't know if that's a workable little girl's name these days."

"Well, who knew Mabel and Maude would come back?" Tad offered as assurance.

He saw on a side table a candlelit menorah, and was reminded again that the Baums were Jewish, though it was never emphasized in the press coverage he remembered from his childhood. Beneath the menorah, confusingly, were strewn piles of green and red Christmas gifts, some opened, some not. "I see you've already made some headway with the presents!" he remarked. He'd learned from Bonny that hosts like guests who pay attention to the surroundings.

"They're from people we mostly don't even know!" Ruth laughed, fishing a crystal bud vase out of a nest of wood shaving. "Look at the engraving. *Slashers 2!*"

"It's a promotional gift from the producers," Minus explained merrily. He and Ruth enlisted Tad in laughing at the odd, impersonal corporate gifts they'd received from her still-video-vigorous dad's distributors, lawyers, and agency. The couple was particularly entertained by a bottle of champagne that, weirdly, had been dipped in chocolate. Tad noticed that Ruth and Minus seemed to take their rarefied privilege with a sense of its absurdity.

"Oh, look at this!" To continue the comic show-and-tell, Minus led Tad to a side table. "We told Anna she could pick any holiday cake she wanted at the bakery! Look at the one she selected!" There was a buxom fashion-doll figure in a Santa hat, with a huge billowing hoop skirt made of cake and frosted to resemble ermine-trimmed red velvet. "Who is she, anyway? Santa's *mistress*?"

Ruth shook her head. "We try to raise her with gender-neutral fairness, but despite the karate lessons, and the picture books about how the lioness does the actual hunting, she still gravitates to the dolls and the makeup! Now she wants to take ballet! Me, I think it's a form of ritual bondage, all that excruciating tiptoeing! It's like they've been tied up and are trying to get to the phone to call the police!" Tad was pleasantly surprised to hear her free-associate with him. She sensed her possible filibuster, and sweetly defused it. "Oh, I don't know. I'm from circus folk."

"Look at this!" Minus added playfully, and lifted the doll's torso. It was an attachment to the cake, legless. "No bottom!

She's like a prop. Anna was so disappointed when she saw that! She thought there was an entire doll in there. We told her it could be her doll that's standing up to her waist in an imaginary swimming pool, and she sort of accepted that. She's got other gifts to look forward to, anyway. But it reminds me how those old Victorian skirts were supposed to convince you that women were too virtuous to have private parts!"

"Would you like something to drink, Tad?" Ruth asked. "We have glögg."

Minus grinned—the old snaggletoothed grin that Tad nonetheless found attractive—and now mimed guzzling from a bottle. "As in *glug glug glug!*"

"It's not as disgusting as eggnog," Ruth offered as a deadpan recommendation. "And I've even got some Mogen David in case Elijah shows up!"

"Uh, white wine?" Tad responded. He remembered Dad once advising him to drink only one variety of alcohol to minimize a hangover. The wisdom of our forefathers.

Ruth left the room, and Minus gazed after her with satisfaction. From another room came Anna's voice. "Daddy! I can't get the Scotch tape to work!"

"Excuse me, Tad!" Minus said. "My wicked empress is calling me. Coming, *gumman!*"

Tad noticed on the nearby grand piano, among a Stonehenge of framed family photos, a dated but impressive picture of craggy Magnus Persson and his wife, Christine Larsen, on a windswept winter beach. Both wore fisherman's sweaters, the kind whose thick-knit patterns are supposed to identify you even if you decompose after drowning. Minus, once so seamless and sunny, now looked pleasantly weather-beaten, like his father.

There was another photo near it, a fading color studio shot of a pretty prepubescent girl with curly hair, slightly too much of it, in the early seventies white Afro fashion. He assumed it was Ruth, and then he saw the inscription: "Ruth, you're the purtiest gal in the zoo! Love always and then some, Dadsy." In smaller writing was a contrite addition. "P.S. Sorry to miss your big day!"

He saw on the wall behind the piano a framed sampler that, in the dim light, seemed to read GOD BLESS OUR FAME. A closer examination revealed it to be the more conventional GOD BLESS OUR HOME.

Tad listened to the contented fire consume itself. If Magnus Persson and Christine Larsen were slightly famous to the intellectual fringe, Bobsy Baum was flat-out famous, recognized by undemanding millions around the world. Even Tad's mom knew who Bobsy was, but she couldn't have identified Gunnar Sternland. Bobsy's most successful film had been the Cold War–era fantasy *The Humans Race,* in which the chubby little coward character he always played was accidentally part of a rocket trip to Mars. Somehow the superrace of Martians—with their distinctly Russian accents—pit themselves in a high-stakes interplanetary Olympics against Bobsy and his friend, the hero astronaut (only in a Bobsy Baum movie would a leading man play the supporting role). Through coincidence and actual climactic bravery, Bobsy wins one for earth and mankind is saved. At the fade-out, he's embracing a greenish girl with four arms and saying into the spaceship's radio, "Mother? There's someone I'd like you to meet. . . ." Apparently, the men Martians were bad and the women Martians were nice, or compliant anyway. Tad had loved the picture as a child watching reruns, and now here he was in earth's pretend savior's daughter's home.

Anna could be heard crying, and Minus was trying to calm her. "Now now, Anna. Remember little Lord Jesus, away in the manger? 'No crying he makes'?"

Ruth came back in with a glass of wine. She handed it to Tad but called into the other room, "Honey? I thought we were going to try to minimize the little Lord Jesus!" She lowered her voice to speak confidentially to Tad, a compliment, since she barely knew him. "'No crying he makes!'

Jesus as the original suffer-in-silence role model! Jesus died! Aren't you sorry you're healthy? You'd think Jesus was a Jewish mother. *'I'll just sit here in the dark, making no crying!'* " She shrugged and picked up her own half-empty glass of seltzer. Tad hadn't expected, from this trim and pretty woman, echoes of her gross father's performing style. She interpreted his surprise as disagreement. "Oh my! No offense. Minus says you're studying God, but he said you don't believe in Him."

"Oh, I don't! Not at all!" He assured her fervently, which seemed to please her.

"Well, here's to . . ." She grinned and lifted her seltzer, but was at a loss for a toast.

"Imaginary beings!" Tad offered. "Ourselves included!"

"Oh, that sounds like Bishop Berkeley malarkey!" Ruth commented. *Malarkey* was a perfect Bobsy Baum word, Tad noted. "Life is but a dream? If only!"

Minus returned, happily shaking his head. "Well! Grandma's gift is going to be completely covered in Scotch tape! We could leave it out in the rain without a worry!" Tad turned to face him. "You *must* have children, Taddeus! It is the greatest! Carrying them on your shoulder, teaching them proper Scotch tape use! I know it might require negotiation, but do it!" Tad could see Minus's thought patterns wash over his face like an innocent adult who changes his clothes with the window shades up. He was recalling Tad's foray into his sister. "Oh! Speaking of . . . I mean, Tad, I have a surprise for you!"

"Inger's coming?"

Minus stared, then laughed. "Yes, she's staying with us for a few days! How did you guess?"

"I don't know, I guess I anticipated it. And it is the season for it."

"And our mother is here, too! They're here to shop! They're almost never in New York! You've never met my mother, have you?"

"Well, I did, only briefly. When I was, as it were, dating Inger, she came through Boston on a movie promotion and took her out to dinner."

"Well well! And why not you, too?"

"I think she offered to, but . . . I don't remember anymore. We were already having problems."

"Ah, convoluted youth," Minus reminisced. "So difficult! I'm much less complex now. And here's our Anna!" His tiny daughter came into the room, wearing a black velvet dress that matched her mother's, and a glittering plastic tiara. The firelight on her face reminded Tad that supposedly the cherubim were ruddy-cheeked because they reflected the glory of the God they faced.

"This is the empress I was telling you about," Minus whispered histrionically. "She got it as a present this morning and now she won't take it off! Anna, can you say hello to Tad?"

"Hello," the child said cautiously.

"It's nice to meet you, Your Majesty," Tad smiled and took her hand lightly. "You're the queen, is that right?"

"Yes, that's right," she answered matter-of-factly.

"I've got a nephew who's also into ruling everything. Maybe you should get together. And where are you the queen of?" Tad asked.

Her Serene Highness had a momentary loss of serenity, but after a moment her frozen eyes reanimated. "I don't know," she answered, though without sounding too worried about it. "Yet."

"Well, if you're free to pick," Minus postulated, "you might as well make it someplace very big!"

"Dreamland's pretty big," Tad suggested.

"Ah yes, Dreamland!" Minus grinned. "Where you've been working as a resident alien." Even after several years apart, he seemed to read Tad like a book, and a book for junior readers at that.

"Mmmm," acceded Tad. "Elsewhere? I'm there!"

"There's no such place really," advised Anna. "I've been to a lot of places in planes. I know."

"They're just playing, Anna," Ruth said softly. "Like when you have your stuffed giraffe talk. It isn't real talking." Tad couldn't tell if Ruth meant that the conversation or the speakers were unreal.

"What do you want for Christmas, Anna?" Tad asked.

"A giraffe," she answered calmly.

"She's currently obsessed with giraffes," Minus explained. "My theory is that they combine the typical horse craze with the typical ballerina craze."

"She even cut the picture of the giraffe out of the encyclopedia! I don't know how she thought she wouldn't get caught!" Ruth grinned and stroked Anna's hair. Clearly the transgression had been forgiven long ago.

"Then she taped it on the wall by her bed!" Minus continued. Obviously, Anna saw Scotch tape as a means to power.

"Because I wanted to have it. In the book, it wasn't mine," Anna explained, a little annoyed her parents were telling a stranger about her illicit romance. Tad understood her possessiveness. Some lovers aren't content to leave their sweethearts in the encyclopedia; they try to put them in a separate place. "The giraffe is the biggest animal there is," Anna went on, as if to explain her infatuation.

"Well, actually . . ." Tad debated contradicting a child. "It is the tallest. The elephant is the biggest. Of *land* animals, anyway."

"Ooh!" Ruth overacted finding these facts interesting. "Tad knows all about the animal kingdom!" She was trying to sell Tad to Anna. Her word choice reminded Tad that folklorists and even scientists choose to organize the animal world into a kingdom.

"The *whale* is the biggest of all animals," Tad continued.

"People tend to forget about the whale because it's in the ocean, and the people making the lists are on land, so they think land is more important."

This got a confused silent response from Minus and Ruth, but Anna was now involved in the debate.

"Then what's the *tallest* ocean animal?" she asked.

Tad took her seriously. "Well, that's a little trickier, because nobody's standing up in the ocean, they're mostly sideways. You know, swimming. So we talk about how *long* they are instead."

Minus feigned astonishment. "You've got the very biosphere stratified!" He stooped to match his daughter's height and began to tickle her, which she both resisted and encouraged.

Tad had mixed feelings of envy and pleasure at his good friend's jet stream of a life, his rare peaceful disposition, his loving marriage, their firelight. Their appealing daughter made him review his chimerical desire for children, for fatherhood and family, and the weird molestation charge that muddled this mirage. He then guiltily thought of Angelo. Angelo was like his favorite lowbrow comic book, a guilty, comfortable pleasure he'd put aside, presuming a great text like one of Milton's was due him, even though, like Dean Parish, those could be difficult to read. Genuinely fun comic books and partners should be prized.

Minus had picked up his guitar—the very one he and Tad had sung to in coffeehouses—and, as a private joke, began to strum through a Swedish carol both he and Tad had always found weirdly literal. In translation, it had seemingly moronic lyrics:

> *Christmas is here again, Christmas is here again,*
> *And it's going to last 'til Easter!*
> *No, that can't be true! No, no, that can't be true—*
> *Because, before Easter, Lent comes.*

Ouch, Tad reflected. Those cold-weather types—which arguably include the Irish, if you go with the Viking rape stories—can't let go of Lent. An umlaut of guilt hovers over their Ho Ho. Even their version of the infant Saint Nicholas supposedly refused his mother's nipple on fast days. For Tad himself, this year, Lent had come before Christmas. Did that mean after Christmas, Easter would come?

Minus continued, as if serenading Anna. "'I saw three ships come sailing in, on Christmas Day, on Christmas Day . . .'" Tad remembered Minus's enthusiasm for old melodies, how they'd sung twee glee club throwbacks like "Glorious Apollo" or "Good Claret Is My Mistress Now," a drinking song about a scornful puss denying her swain.

Minus hadn't cared that he was partnered onstage with a gay man. When Tad had asked him if he minded being mistaken for gay, Minus had shrugged and said, "I can't help what people think. If I were Jewish, and some people looked down on me for being Jewish, would that make me less of a man? You live as best you can, no matter what the ignorant think. Your Eleanor Roosevelt said something about how no one can belittle you without your cooperation." Minus spoke English with greater exactitude than most native English speakers, and was more accepting of Tad's gayness than Tad was himself.

"Such a lovely carol," Ruth said dreamily. "Though what the heck the three boats have to do with anything beats me."

Anna looked curious. "How are *carols* different from songs?"

Minus paused in his playing. "No one knows," he answered with lighthearted gravity.

Tad's mind was unaccountably seized with an image of Inger, not a memory, exactly, because he hadn't witnessed it. It was of Inger as a teen, wearing Saint Lucia Day candles. They had caused her hair to catch fire, leading to her having her head close-cropped and then playing Saint Joan at her

Geneva boarding school. It had all grown back by the time Tad met her.

Suddenly, there she was, Valkyrie Inger, stamping snow off her boots in the vestibule like Artemis back from the hunt, only instead of venison, she carried bags from assorted boutiques.

"Hello!" she called. *Yo ho, tow ho!* She was now as big as a nice house, and, Tad knew, had a husband and two daughters in Seattle. She put down her parcels, and took a deep breath when she saw Tad, as if she'd just lifted a lovely but breakable gift out of its nest of tissue.

"My costly one!" she beamed, going to him without removing her overcoat. They'd met in freshman French class, and always made a joke of the fact that *cher* meant both "darling" and "expensive."

"Nice to see you!" He hugged her, and the melting snow on her coat made his shirtsleeves wet. Her blond hair, not so lustrous now, was short, like Ruth's, but not severe. Tad's anxiety about seeing her now seemed unnecessary. Perhaps her overweight humanized her, leveled the field, the way Gabe's smoking made him seem less unreachable.

"We're in town for only a few days, to *shop.*"

Her sleek, slightly accented voice brought back memories of his undergraduate torment and happiness. "*Shop*—that is such a northern European verb, at least the way you say it!" he mused.

She answered saucily, as if she were touching him on each syllable. "Like *ship*? Or *slop*? *Slip. Sleep. Stop.*" He remembered how galvanizingly healthy she'd been at eighteen, how unkempt Waterville Tad had lit into her rosy grace like an orphan with a spoon attacking mounds of strawberry shortcake.

"You're in a playful mood," he observed with relief.

"Well! Free, however briefly, of my beloved husband and delightful children, I feel absolutely weightless!" She smiled.

"How's doctoring?"

"Good!" she said intensely, as if relishing mountain air. "I love running others' lives!" She'd been a weapons-research scientist, Tad knew from Minus, but after her first child was born, she'd felt her job was immoral and then went to medical school instead. Only all-powerful Inger could have done that. Even her plumpness was a sign of her mastery of the situation, no matter what convention called for.

Anna had run into the kitchen and started some commotion that also took Minus and Ruth out of the living room. Anna could be heard simulating the tears of the wronged, a tired child having a tantrum. "Time out!" Ruth was saying. "Time out!"

Inger and Tad were briefly alone together. "So you are now a full-bore thirty-second-degree bohemian?" she teased.

"Yeah." Tad grinned, deciding this exquisite creature deserved his full honesty. "I, uh, turned out to be gay and everything."

She smiled, that Scandinavian "mulling brandy in your mouth" pucker that he always found so worldly. "I'm not surprised that you're gay," she offered smoothly. "But I am surprised that you're *everything*. I always thought that was only God's . . . prerogative."

She'd playfully mocked any possible tension here, and reflected her family's Nordic tradition of God-fearing atheism. "I was going to say 'terrain,' but that didn't seem like . . . enough!"

Contemplating the aplomb of this huge kittenish woman, Tad, to his own surprise, recalled a scene from another of Bobsy's fantasy comedies, a burlesque called *Jerk and the Beanstalk*. In it, the giant's wife had not been an ogress, but, rather, a fifty-foot babe in a negligee. When Bobsy as Jack declared his intention to make love to her, she had famously answered, "If you do, I just better not find out about it!" He realized with a start that the glacial movie giantess was Ruth's mom, who later died in a car crash in the middle of her divorce proceedings.

"Are you here through New Year's?"

"Just until the day after tomorrow. My husband's in Aspen teaching our daughters to ski, and I thought I'd slalom down Fifth Avenue instead."

"Inger! When's Christine arriving?" Minus asked as he returned and gingerly removed his sister's coat.

"She said she'd be here at seven."

"She could have stayed here, too. We have extra rooms." Minus seemed to be repeating a refrain he'd spoken many times. Tad mentally filed the fact about the extra rooms, though he secretly embarrassed himself, to be conniving about exploiting people he loved. "But, you know *Christine,*" Minus spoke his mother's first name as if to identify one of her assorted personalities. "Peasants stay with relatives. Well-bred people stay in hotels." He and Inger headed to the kitchen, to greet Ruth and Anna and to get Inger some glögg.

Alone, Tad remembered his breakup with Inger, in which she seemed to understand already facts he himself couldn't face. He'd praised her long blond hair, and she'd gone out and gotten it all cut off. It was a gesture of independence or defiance, like a scene in her parents' movies about inexplicably embattled couples, where even compliments and lovely presents were analyzed for awful ulterior motives. Tad had startled himself when he found he was far more turned on by her new boyish look, but the breakup was imminent. He couldn't remember what he'd said last year to extricate himself from Angelo—because he'd been the villain and didn't wish to relive it—but he remembered, after sixteen years, every word of Inger's careful disengagement.

"It's not happening, somehow," she'd said the night before exam period was to begin.

"But I always reach orgasm, don't I?" he'd answered defensively.

"Yes, you do, but it's like your projected goal, instead of the fabulous revelation that ends the play. I don't like being an objective. You aren't thinking about me. Other men I've slept with are less intent to, as it were, prove the point. It's like when my parents have to play love scenes in their films. They may undress, they may press their bodies against other actors, they must make it believable to the audience, but they know not to believe it in their hearts. I don't know, you don't believe this, somehow. You aren't here. It's like being with a ghost. A ghost who's haunting the wrong house."

The front door opened again, and Minus hurried from the kitchen to greet their next guest. There in three dimensions was Christine Larsen, in a turban, the supposedly elegant accessory matrons affect to indicate their transition from princess to maharani. Tad had met her momentarily sixteen years earlier, when she was visiting Inger, but now Inger looked like her then, and she looked as if advancing age were a spell cast on her definitive 1960s self by a rival star. Behind her trailed a cowed-looking taxi driver carrying a large cellophane-wrapped fruit basket.

"Hello! Hello!" She hugged everyone but Tad, whom she didn't remember, but she gave him a dazzling smile. "Isn't this place lovely?"

"We rented it sight unseen!" Minus seemed proud of his and Ruth's intuition for real estate.

Ruth appeared and asked in courteous counterpoint, "How's the hotel, Christine?"

"Fine, fine. I didn't like my first room, but they moved me and sent me a fruit basket. I'm only here for a few days, and I'm not going to eat it, so here it is." The taxi driver set it in the doorway and left, bewildered, a blameless zombie in the clothes he'd been buried in.

"How did you get the cabdriver to carry that all the way into the house?" Minus asked, marveling as he moved the huge basket to a less obstructive corner. "They don't do that in New York."

Christine smiled innocently. "Don't they? I told him to and he just did." She had an air of certainty that seemed to compel accommodation. "Where's little Anna?"

Ruth laughed. "Didn't you hear her? I just had her lie down for a minute. She's *tired*." She gave the word such implied significance, it reminded Tad of Mom describing Dad after a party: "He's *tired*."

"I'd love a glass of wine," Christine announced, a touch of the hotel guest lingering in her delivery. "Beaujolais nouveau, if you have it!"

"We do!" Minus played the crisp steward.

Christine addressed Tad, since, as the one nonfamily member, he was the one to be seduced. "I always regard the arrival of the Beaujolais nouveau as the beginning of Christmastime!" Tad was attracted by her fame as much as anything.

Minus went to fetch the wine, and Christine announced, "The picture of his father! It is too bad Magnus couldn't make it! He's playing yet another Nazi in a movie that's filming in Czechoslovakia." She dropped her overcoat on the floor dramatically and sat in the living room's largest chair. "He likes to say that World War Two was very hard on his childhood, but it's being very good to him in his old age!" As Ruth took Christine's coat, Tad noticed it was mink. He was bemused, but he figured, like Magnus, childhood hardship entitled her to her choice of status in age. *I wear the furs I forged in life.*

"Remember Tad Leary, Mother?" Inger said, with the only hint of deference Tad had ever heard in her voice. "You met him my freshman year? And then he and Minus became a musical team."

"I always talked about him, remember?" Minus gave her some wine and added his letter of recommendation. "He's the only full-fledged New Yorker here!"

"I remember you, of course!" Christine smiled. "From the courtyard, under that great oak! The moment I saw you, I thought to myself, This is Inger's boyfriend? How can this be? He is a homosexual!" She added a sample of her tinkling laughter to indicate how charming this was meant to be, rather than tactless. Tad inwardly wondered which he preferred, his own mother's silence on sexual matters or Inger's mother's astonishing straightforwardness.

Similarly, in college, he had been amazed at the notion of one's own mother rolling naked before millions of people, as Christine so often had in her films. Her typical scenario had involved undressed pillow talk between lover opponents whose love and hate oscillated more quickly than a skittish stock market, and usually required suicide as a proof of commitment. Audiences had gazed at her creamy skin while she recited Sternland's long monologues about anomie and self-loathing. Now, of course, this goddess had entered the third phase of her trinity, having moved from nymph to queen to crone. Tad had just seen her as one of the horrifyingly made-up Fates in a new American movie depicting the legend of Perseus and Medusa, only in this version Perseus had been recast as Hercules, presumably because American audiences had never heard of Perseus. Christine, once an international fantasy object, was required, courtesy of special effects, to remove her eyeball and pass it on, which had caused groans at the screening Tad attended. He decided not to mention this disputable achievement.

For her sake, he brought up a prouder moment as he sat down. "*Frost and Ashes* was on public television the other night. It really is an intense experience!"

Christine smiled ironically. "*Frost and Ashes*! Ah, yes! That title doesn't offer many options, does it? But I was so young, and it was a challenge to play, well, lovesickness, syphilis, madness, and frostbite, all at the same time." She made it sound like a recipe. Tad remembered seeing the picture sixteen years earlier, with Inger, when it had been revived at the Art Cinema near Hale, and how guiltily excited he'd been to be dating the genetic extension of a famous couple. Christine's character was a novitiate in a remote island nunnery who goes slowly mad, starting with inappropriate barefootedness and building up to sleeping in puddles, crying during sex, and seeing the face of God in a polished spoon. It was the character's own distorted reflection, of course, and in college Tad had thought that was pretty cosmic.

"It certainly proved that blondes don't necessarily have more fun!" Tad tried to joke, but when he got a blank stare from Christine, he remembered she wouldn't recognize an old American ad jingle.

"There's no one like Gunnar Sternland making pictures today!" Ruth put in dutifully, rescuing Tad and currying favor with her mother-in-law. *Whither thou goest with this conversation, I will go.*

"Oh, Sternland. His people were all clergymen, that's why his films are dripping with God. He wasn't some vulgarian out of vaudeville!" Christine added her tinkling laugh again, as if it were an antiseptic that removed the sting, and Tad looked uneasily to see if Ruth was offended at this reference to her father's world. Tad was light-headed in this upper atmosphere, where someone could be in the position of looking down on America's most beloved comedy icon. Either from good sportsmanship or good manners, Ruth simply smiled inscrutably. Vaudeville, Tad surmised, was her father's version of having fought in World War II, and he had been proud to have survived it.

"We can have dinner anytime—it's all ready," Ruth said helpfully, since dinner guests wait for instruction. Then she seemed to answer Christine's comment. "Well, you know, my father's father was a circus clown, and my father had a wonderful success, but he was always a little ashamed that he wasn't a circus clown, too. I think he thought that the circus was pure, and that the movies were a kind of, I don't know, opportunism, a compromise with technology."

They headed to the dining room table. "It's all relative," Tad said, attempting to agree with both sides. "Martin Luther wasn't impressed with Popes."

"Appealing to my Protestant side!" Christine laughed. "I meant no criticism of comedy. And it is true that Swedes are too serious, you know. My parents were Danish, they knew how to laugh. They were—how shall I put this?—connected to the Continent, you see what I mean?" Young Tad had never imagined intramural Scandinavian prejudices until Inger mentioned her father considered Laplanders the equivalent of hillbillies.

As they seated themselves around the table, Tad remembered movie images of Christine starving or screaming, and he tried to reconcile it with this chic, complacent grandmother. "Did you ever experience the kind of anguish and despair the characters you played did?" he asked.

"Ohhhhh . . ." Christine gazed into her sea-dark wine as if she saw tropical fish just beneath the surface. "Anguish and despair are fine for the movies, but real life is a little more fun."

Ruth had brought in several covered dishes of grilled fish and vegetables. "Serve yourselves, folks!" she announced. "We don't stand on ceremony here!" Tad noticed that, despite their presumed wealth, Ruth apparently cooked and served everything herself.

"You know, in Britain," Minus began. He often began sentences that way. For some reason, he was smitten with Britain. "On Christmas, the army officers serve the enlisted men their meal! It's a sort of topsy-turvy day!"

"I see. Give the Powerless a Break Day." Tad sounded as if he was translating into English, or, more exactly, American. "The hierarchies are lowered!"

When everyone was served, Ruth poured herself a tiny bit of wine. "To Magnus!" she said, toasting her absent father-in-law, and Tad marveled at her insightful social skills.

"To my darling ex!" Christine proclaimed, to turn the moment from Magnus's to hers. She must have noticed Tad's confusion, and she leaned toward him as if to tell a joke. "We're divorced, but we live together," she explained. It was a modern twist Tad had not encountered before. "We were much too young when we got divorced. It was just what everyone else was doing! I tell you, don't divorce impetuously. Wait to make sure the hate is real!"

They ate in silence for a moment, and Tad noticed Ruth's untypical far-off expression. He wondered if she was recalling her own parents' more famous separation.

"How are all those lawsuits coming along?" Christine resumed, as if on cue. She was fearless, though as an actress, it wasn't clear if that was by design or nature.

Ruth sighed. "Please! I'm giving myself the night off from thoughts about courtrooms!"

Nonetheless, as the meal progressed, she obligingly described the latest in her family's legal problems. Ruth and Minus's lot had seemed perfect to Tad, in this home-sampler sample, but apparently Bobsy, despite his pop-eyed childish sissy image, had been an assiduous womanizer and had fathered many children out of wedlock, that stiffly one-use word. Lawsuits from claimants of all ages (over twelve) constantly nipped at her daily life and her inheritance as his supposedly only child. Tad was reminded that the male gets away with whatever he can, and despite his daisy-clutching vulnerability in *Hoboes in the Hoosegow,* Bobsy had been as ravenously promiscuous as any bum given the opportunity would be. As Tad would.

"The worst part," Ruth concluded, "is that if they are my real half sisters or half brothers, I'd like to get to know them! I don't want to fight them in court. The problem is, a lot of them have proved to be completely phony! It's just exhausting!"

"They want her to write a book!" Minus announced, as if he found the idea both impressive and hilarious.

"Yes." Ruth played at grimness. "Except they want a Daddy Did Me book and I don't want to do that. My father had his faults—ho boy, did he—but he tried hard, and my family life is not my neighbors' business. Besides, you don't betray your own bloodline. What if Anna wrote a book about us?"

Tad thought of his dad, who might have made a good vaudevillian himself, judging by his wild impromptu bedtime stories. Dad, who had taken him to all those Red Sox games Tad was wildly bored by, but still, Dad had once made an effort. And unlike Bobsy, there was no evidence he had ever been unfaithful to Mom, unless unconsciousness could be considered a rival.

Anna had appeared in the doorway, a crabby expression making her beautiful face funny. "I don't want to write a book!" she said in fright, as if some unexpected preschool homework assignment had fallen out of the sky.

"That's good, sweetie!" Ruth touched her daughter's red hair bow, and Tad wondered if that feminine curlicue had been at Anna's insistence. "Go say hi to Grandma." The word *grandma* seemed incongruous applied to Christine, but once Anna sat in her lap, she looked the part. She began whispering loving nonsense into Anna's ears, about how the Yule elf Tomten would soon be coming to visit her. It freed the rest of the group to converse.

"What I proposed," Ruth resumed, "was a book about my grandparents, the Tannenbaums." Bobsy must have shortened his name, Tad reasoned. Then he remembered in slight confusion that the name also meant "Christmas tree." "He was the clown, and she made costumes for the circus."

"How beautiful," Tad answered sincerely, and it occurred to him that circuses were another virtually imaginary place that must have bizarre power hierarchies. Do the aerialists look down on the clowns, besides literally? Is the ringmaster a nobody offstage? Was there anti-Semitism in the turn-of-the-century circus world? Is there still?

"But they don't think the grandparents will sell," Minus explained with mixed resignation and amusement.

"You must come out to our real house in Whitehaven," Ruth continued, flushing with pride. "I mean, the one I lived in as a child. She—my grandmother—collected buttons. I never knew her—my dad was sixty when I was born—but I found them among her things, and I had them all framed under glass like rare beetles or butterflies. These were mostly from circus costumes, so you can imagine how extravagant-looking a lot of them are!"

"I love collections!" Tad enthused. "They make subjects seem *manageable*."

"The fact that I never met her makes me want to reach out and connect with her, somehow. That helped me feel I was doing that. The book would help me do that. Are your parents alive?" Ruth asked Tad.

Tad thought of Dad's motionless nap earlier in the day, and Mom's sitting alongside, the pharaoh's wife obligingly following into the tomb. "Not really," he said vaguely.

Ruth looked confused, which made Tad feel abashed. "I'm sorry," he corrected himself. "They are alive! My mind drifted."

"Tad's mind *drifts*," Minus explained. "He's a . . . a *psychonaut*!" He looked pleased to land on this word, and poured himself and Tad more white wine. "And you, Hansel? How are things in your Black Forest?" He tapped his fingertips on his own temples, indicating dark inner hemispheres.

"Well, I think the new principal at Excelsior is going to do some restructuring. . . ." Tad thought he'd unveil his distress in stages.

"Uh-oh!" Ruth's ready sound effects proved she was her father's legitimate heir.

"Yes." Tad left his half-lie unfinished to minimize the sin of it. "And I'm about to get kicked out of my sublet. The actor

I'm renting from is coming back to town." It occurred to Tad that even though he had abandoned acting, he still seemed to associate with nothing but actors. He liked their readiness to flee reality, as a career choice.

"Oh! Those traveling players!" Minus pretended to be outraged.

"Is there no sweetheart for you to move in with?" Inger asked. Tad appreciated the fact that she was so at ease on this subject. The Learys generally left it untouched.

"No, all alone." Tad shrugged and sipped his wine. He then noted with annoyance at himself that it was his own doing, after all, and added, "But I'm not even looking!"

"That's when it happens!" Inger pointed out. "When you aren't looking for it!"

"Well, I think there's some reverse reverse psychology at work here. I intentionally stop looking for it, so God sees me not looking for it, and says Oh no! I see what you're up to!" It seemed foolish even to Tad, and they all laughed. Romance was the least of his worries. Besides, sitting there, it occurred to him that porno videos were a better substitute for actual sex than broadcast television was for the actual company of friends.

"Ahh!" Minus grinned. "So, *Good Claret Is Your Mistress Now.*"

"Well, yes." Wine was certainly caressing Tad at that moment. He had recited his secret problems, but they seemed trivial in this sweet company.

"Well, add boils and we've got the Book of Job!" Minus said breezily. At that free-floating moment, Tad couldn't recall any boils in Job.

Anna was dozing on her grandmother's lap. "I'll take her, Christine," Ruth offered.

"No, no!" Christine protested. "It seems I was holding Inger like this only yesterday!"

"If you really were, you'd be in hospital now!" Inger joked. Tad was briefly confused by self-deprecation from such a successful woman. Her overweight was her shortness.

"She needs to go to bed," said Ruth, standing.

"I'll put her down," offered Inger. "She's my godchild."

"Or I can," said Christine. Maternity impressed Tad as a fraternity more unifying than paternity, or, for that matter, fraternity. The three women left the room together, with now fully demythicized Christine carrying Anna, the queen of somewhere.

"Ah! The ladies have left us!" Minus observed, and, accordingly, proffered a box of cigars. Tad declined, but Minus lit up and the two men sat alone at the table for a few minutes. They idly joked about how the courses of the standard dinner compared to the course of evolution on earth. Soup followed by salad, a fish or meat course, and then dessert and cigars was—with some bending—analagous to the primordial sea, vegetation, fishes, mammals, and, with the coming of man, artificial stuff that's not necessary, and pollution.

They laughed at their theory's uselessness, then sat in silence. Tad heard the dying fire pop unexpectedly in the other room. Minus stirred in his chair. "Ah, Tad! What am I to do?" he said, smiling, but with a sheepish sigh. "I am a hedonist, and alas, I can afford to be one!"

Tad then knew he loved Minus sincerely, since he wasn't jealous of his friend's comfort. "Hey, perhaps you could study yourself as a thesis subject! That could make hedonism a kind of work."

Minus smiled at the idea and at the fact that he didn't have to do any such thing. "By the way . . . I don't mean to play the condescending gentleman," he said, taking advantage of the fact that he and Tad were alone, "but that house in Whitehaven goes unoccupied and vulnerable to robbers about half the time. Ruth will be busy in court, and I'll be busy . . .

doing . . . whatever it is I do!" His aimlessness was *his* short-ness. "Besides the main house, there's a guest house by the pool. Perhaps you could be our housesitter."

"It's like, a manger?"

"Exactly. Whatever that is. You can be the Holy Child, or if that's too much pressure—and, also, I know you hate getting mistaken for a little boy—you can be one of the shepherds, or that odd fellow from 'Silent Night.' You know—Round John Virgin!"

Tad was touched, but he wondered if this meant gardening chores or changing fuses. "Would I need any special skills, like with electricity or plumbing?"

"I suppose there might be caretaker's duties involved, as well," Minus confessed hesitantly. "Ruth knows more about it than I do." He proceeded to describe a sequence of technical security tasks Tad's ears typically and resolutely denied entry. Eventually, Minus finished the portion of his speech that was foreign to Tad. "But it's very rustic, very peaceful. You could do your schoolwork."

Tad was uneasy at the prospect of becoming a tenant and employee of his best friend. Besides, Tad didn't like either hard work or nature.

"Can I think about this?"

"Of course," Minus said. "And I should consult Ruth first, of course. But there's another position I wish to offer you, as well. It, too, would be unpaid."

"What?"

"Will you stand as godfather to our Esther?" He sounded slightly impulsive and eager to comfort.

Tad felt simultaneous delight and distress. Nat and Les had traded the godfather accolades for their sons, and Tad thought they'd made the prudent brotherly selection. Still, he wondered now if Minus was trying to make him feel better, if this were artifical rain on a movie set, to save make-believe sharecroppers from strictly imaginary starvation. "That would be a wonderful honor!" he said, more confused than usual. "But I don't have any money, I couldn't put her through college or pay for her braces."

"We don't need your money!" Minus laughed. "She'll be all set in any case. I mean it. You'd make a fine father figure. It just wouldn't be actual size."

"I'm glad you think so, but it's like saying you'd be brave in a lifeboat. You don't know what you'll do until you're in that situation." Tad always loved playing with children, but it was a relief when they were taken away to be disciplined by others and raised at others' expense.

"Well, parenthood isn't a constantly sinking ship!" argued Minus. "It's more like"—his college essay experience made him determined to find a clean parallel—"a ship where you're recreation director, chef, stoker, and captain all at once at all times. And it's a motorboat."

"That doesn't sound much easier."

"It isn't. But it's better."

"I'd love to be your daughter's godfather," Tad said, the breadth of Minus's gesture dawning on him. Then he remembered with a thud his discharge from Excelsior. It pained him to ruin one of his life's most honorable moments, but it would have been dishonorable not to. "I should tell you something, though," he began slowly. "They just fired me from Excelsior because this one woman thought I was . . . touching her son. It isn't true, though."

"Well, it isn't true. End of untrue story."

Ruth returned alone and sat as best her enlarged self could on Minus's lap.

"Anna told me to say good night to the little boy who knows all about animals!" She smiled at Tad.

"All About Animals!" Tad mused. "There's a title for you."

"I asked Tad to be Esther's godfather," Minus told Ruth cautiously.

Ruth looked mildly surprised, which Tad figured meant she was quite surprised. "Oh! Well, very good!" She finally shrugged, which Tad might have taken as a slight, except it meant she was green-lighting him. Apparently, she was adept at sailing with her husband. Again, it was incongruous to see this sleek woman volunteer shtick. It reminded Tad of Bobsy's shrug to the camera at the fade-out of *Married Alive,* when he realizes at the altar it's his delectable new bride who's the murderess.

Tad tried to anticipate valid criticism. "I told Minus I was a bum."

"No problem!" Ruth said. "I myself have no . . . well, no *official* sisters and brothers. Anyway, I have no intention of dying in the next twenty years."

"And besides," Minus added, "for insurance, we'll get someone *really good* to be godmother. Remember, though," he warned, "at the christening, you'll have to renounce the devil and all his works."

Christine appeared in the doorway, the older image of her own granddaughter minutes earlier. "I'm still on European time," she said with a histrionic false yawn. "May I lie down in your spare room?"

"You're welcome to stay the night!" said Ruth promptly.

"No, no," Christine insisted. "I will not. I have my hotel room! I just need to lie down for one minute."

"Of course!" Ruth showed her the way.

"I look forward to meeting you!" Christine called vaguely to Tad as she exited.

Minus shook his head, smiling. "She's a tired girl, too!" he explained.

Tad and Minus toasted the agreement, then relished friendship's silence. When Inger returned, she made a glögg toast, as well.

"It's not a real job, of course," she pointed out when she heard about Tad's godparenthood. "It's like being vice president for five terms."

"I'm just happy to be in Congress," Tad said, remembering as he spoke *congress* was also a funny word for *coitus,* and, after all, any personal interaction, even with demons. Tad felt like curling up and sleeping with this family, but he took that as a warning sign to go.

"Whoa, what a day!" he said, gently detaching himself from his chair. "I should get home."

"Father knows best!" Minus reactivated himself and also stood.

"I'm not a father yet."

"You're always father to your own body! Ushering it around, caring for it, forbidding it to use heroin . . ." Minus wandered out of the room in self-amusement on an unannounced errand.

"It's nice to see you," Inger said simply.

"Same here."

"You must come meet my husband and children, if you ever travel other than astrally." She spoke for a while about them, lovingly, but with increasing fatigue. Tad attributed that to her day's shopping.

Since the meeting was evidently winding up, he thought he'd better clear any old business. "Sorry if I messed you up way back when."

"Oh, Tad." She laughed dismissively. "You had the most thorough inferiority complex of any man I'd ever met. Of course, I was inexperienced then. I've met worse, believe me! Anyway, that's why I slept with you—I thought it would help." She had been the Peace Corps and he was a very tiny country.

"Yes, I know." Tad hugged her. Somehow, this was delightful intimacy rather than disastrous Sternlandian truth telling.

"I'm glad I did. It helped us both grow up, didn't it?"

Tad was typically of two minds about that, but he wanted this parting to be clear tropical sailing. "Absolutely."

"You never hurt me, anyway. It was one more adventure. One more experiment." She and her brother approached life with analytical but unmixed zeal, unlike self-stalemated Tad. She kissed his cheek, the strategic halfway point between lovers' lips and thin air.

"I guess I was just thinking about myself," he admitted.

Inger smiled again. "Well, that's not unique. All men do that. And you forget—our historic affair lasted only three weeks."

It was true, Tad calculated, after doing some hectic mental math. They'd met in French, gotten acquainted, and had broken up before Christmas break. In his memory, it had been Wagnerian. Freshmen live in dog years.

Hosts Ruth and Minus returned with Tad's jacket and joined them at the front door. Inger stood back slightly, since the hosts always have the official last farewell.

"Again, I'm honored about . . ." Tad said, wriggling into his jacket.

"We'll give you the details as they develop!" Minus assured him.

"Bye, Minus. Bye, Ruth!"

"It was good to meet you, after all these years!"

"It'll all work out, you'll see. If not at Whitehaven or here, somewhere else."

"I guess it will!" Tad smiled, momentarily hung in the hammock of happiness. In a maudlin way, he couldn't resist adding, "It's just, I panic whenever I think about my own mortality and the pointlessness of the universe."

Ruth smiled and pretended to be flicking ash off an imaginary cigar. "Well, as my dad used to say in his Doctor Sketch, 'So, don't do that!'"

"I'm in town for the foreseeable future. When the snows recede, we'll go bicycling," Minus pledged. "Will you be around?"

Tad grinned. "Oh, I'm nothing if not around!"

Inger called after him. "This doctor says, 'Get a hat!'"

He started trudging away, and Minus added, "See you anon, betimes, eftsoons!"

Tad marveled at how Oxonian Minus mastered even arcane English vocabulary, but he simultaneously remembered Nat once snorting that anyone who used the word *anon* to be amusing should be shot. Still, if Gabe's smoking made him human and Angelo's awful singing offset his saintliness, then Minus's Anglophilia was at least a classy kind of flaw. And, unlike Simon, Minus wasn't trying to win anything.

Snow was still falling. It had been a lovely dinner, Tad reasoned, and for once he was in full agreement with himself. Then, to his amazement, he saw Donna Silvarini, Angelo's older sibling by less than a year—what Dad referred to as an "Irish twin"—the sister who used to dress Angelo up in her own dresses as if he were her personal dolly. She was pushing a real-life infant in a stroller covered with a transparent plastic tarpaulin to keep out the cold. At first, it reminded Tad of the shabbier houses in Waterville, where instead of fixing glass windows, they hung transparent plastic over them. Then, however, he thought of the miniature greenhouse the Silvarinis maintained behind their house, even though the low-flying planes overhead occasionally shattered the panes. In that part of Waterville, it was a beautiful edifice, a transparent halfway house full of transient flowers.

With Donna was her merchant marine boyfriend, whose name, Tad remembered hastily, was Joseph, but whom his shipmates rechristened Jo Jo, like the Dog-Faced Boy, because his red fiery hair looked a lot like an Irish setter's. Tad always secretly wondered if heavy-browed Jo Jo was one of those males with the extra Y chromosome, who tend to be lurchingly large and disposed to crime. He had been an unsettling presence at Silvarini family parties, since he had habitually carried a pistol and his notion of funny was to answer the phone by saying, "To whom, per*fuck,* am I speaking?" And Donna, who had always been fiercely protective of Angelo, always admonished Tad on parting, "You treat my brother right." That had been bizarre for Tad, the big Italian sister defending her sweet little brother's honor.

"Donna!"

"Tad Leary? My God!" She seemed friendly, and if there was a scintilla of punitive standoffishness in her voice, Tad couldn't decide if it was real or just his paranoid sense of having wronged her favorite doll. She wore an overcoat striped like the rainbow, and in the deep snow under the streetlamp, it seemed a wonderful oasis, although Tad knew it would be sneered at in his onetime lover Dean Parrish's design-conscious crowd.

"Why aren't you in Boston?" Tad asked, realizing as he spoke that he was stereotyping her as a stay-at-home peasant girl.

"We're allowed to cross state borders now, it's really broadening!" she answered, with the level, no-frills self-respect her family had—perennial tomato vines with deep roots. "Joe's sister and her friend live on Jane Street. Joe's folks are dead, so we're having Christmas with them. His sister and her friend, I mean." Tad wondered if the friend alluded to so carefully was a lesbian or a live-in boyfriend.

"I was just thinking about you!" he said. "I was recalling how Angelo said you and he loved your white First Communion outfits so much, you used to go trick-or-treating in them!"

"Yes," she replied, seeming to picture it with pleasure. "Now I wear my bridal gown on Halloween." Her swaddled toddler—gender indeterminable—wore a hooded sweatshirt with soft simulated reindeer horns. "This is little Blitzen."

"Joe junior, actually," Jo Jo corrected with pride. In this fey setting, he seemed mellow, like a bear who's simply been misjudged by the other, more high-strung woodland creatures.

"Oh, you two got married! Congratulations! And you're blessed with issue!"

"Not necessarily in that order." She smiled. Jo Jo rolled his eyes, comically accepting his role as the reluctant boyfriend. "At least my mother didn't live to see a bastard in the family!"

"Oh, but she'd love any grandchild," Tad said with involuntary warmth, even though he worried it might seem dismissive of Jo Jo Junior's specialness. "I mean—" Tad pictured Mrs. Silvarini smoking and weeping as she browsed the family album, beside herself with the depth of her family feeling.

"Yes, she would." Donna corrected herself gently, and returned Tad's warmth for respecting her often-ridiculed mother. Donna and Angelo had once pitched in to buy her an enormous World's Best Mom trophy, which, typically, Tad found an eyesore at first, but then came to admire. "You're right," Donna continued. "Nothing living was illegitimate to her." Tad wondered if that was an allusion to Mrs. Silvarini's automatic acceptance of Tad and Angelo as a couple. He ventured a joke to draw the father into the circle.

"Still packing heat, Jo Jo?"

Jo Jo grinned, as if recalling bygone high jinks. "Not anymore. If anybody messes with me, I'll just throw the baby at them."

They all laughed.

"Yeah, he is big." Tad knew praising a baby's size reassured parents of its chances for survival. "How're the High-Class brothers?"

"Terry's fine, and—oh!—Marco is dating a girl whose last name is Sheehan. We joke that she looks like you with long hair! Family tastes, I guess."

Tad laughed, but he really didn't know how to respond to Donna's observation, except that he knew he didn't want to be likened to a girl. That's my problem, he thought, quickly reprimanding himself, and not Donna's. Besides, red-haired possible extra-Y-chromosomed Jo Jo was part of this equation, as well.

"And how's your dad?" Tad had always admired Mr. Silvarini's habitual silence, as if in solidarity with the vegetation, very unlike Tad's own garrulous father.

"He's still at it! It's inhaling the oxygen from all those plants, Tad. They're starting a huge federal building lobby next month." She paused to check that Joe junior was secure in his stroller. "Anyway, what are you doing thinking about my old Halloween costumes at Christmastime?"

"Well, thinking about Angelo, I guess," Tad said, trying to sound sensitive. Angelo's name had been scrupulously avoided. "It's just about a year since we broke up."

Donna gave him a critical look, but her voice remained friendly. "You mean, since *you* left *him*." Jo Jo simply looked into the street. XYY ultramen don't do soap operas. They're too dangerous.

Tad enacted being cowed, and hunched his shoulders. He had used last New Year's Day as a platform for his underconsidered resolution. Donna now decided to take him off the hook. "Never mind. It's all for the best. You know, he's out in San Francisco now. He's independent, it's great for him." Angelo had been living with his parents before he moved in with Tad, so Donna saw his living alone as an achievement for him, a hallmark of adulthood. "Anyway, we're due for dinner!"

"Yes, me, too!" Tad answered in confusion. He wanted to ask if Angelo was listed in the phone book out there, but half of him told the other half it would be wrong.

"Hey, come see us when you're in Waterville!" Jo Jo said. Tad marveled. A Neanderthal made into a member of society by the powers of fatherhood.

"I will!" Tad grinned as they went on their way. Whether he meant it or not, he sincerely meant to affirm his affection.

"And get a hat!" Donna called back.

Tad noticed that while standing still, falling snow had accumulated in his hair. He shook his head the way a tethered horse kills time. For that moment, the solitude of the dark street was wonderful. Unexpectedly, he felt unfamiliar, uplifting grace descend into him.

6. Twenty Thousand Leagues Out of Your League

At this point, Tad could have gone home satisfied, and, in fact, he should have. Unfortunately, the bliss of the wine and the Perssons' and Silvarinis' teasing but benign acceptance of him, past and present, despite his faults, made him feel benign and forgiving in turn. Self-consciously unlike the wicked steward in the parable who is forgiven a debt by his master but will not forgive his colleague's, Tad wanted to feel expansive, magnanimous, and he considered going back up to the East Side to his one-day stand Dean Parrish's party, to show there were no hard feelings. And secretly—insofar as anyone can have secrets from oneself—he also hoped, against all logic, that Dean might want to sleep with him again, if only one more valedictory time. Tad's penis still eluded capture by his brain.

He was getting what Angelo in his non-Hale way would have called *loopy* now—"Too much Christmas!" as Mom often had to say about Dad on tense December twenty-sixths. After splurging on another, again magically available taxi—the holiday incites people into savoring impulsive expense, like a bungee jump one remembers as clearing the head—he told the driver to head uptown, figuring he could always go back to his provisional home at Garth's. He sat in its dark, "someone else is driving" comfort like a fetus savant and strategized triage on the remaining parties, since he couldn't possibly go to all of them now.

Certainly he could skip the further generic potato chips and secondhand fruitcake at the Alternative School, the downtown college where he now admitted to himself he was only pretending to work on his Ph.D. The Alternative School, Tad grumbled mentally from the Olympian perspective of some but not yet too much wine. Their motto might as well be "When you don't get into the school you really want to go to." His thesis wasn't his reason for living, he pointed out to himself. It was a pretext for loitering. He had dreamed it up as an extra-credit project in a world that wasn't offering him regular credit. Anyway, the department's party, fluorescently lit like an operating room, would just be aesthetic squabbling and Simonized gossip about tenuous tenure, raises that only the microscope could detect, and who published what in journals that no one beside their contributors would ever read. It would be the Excelsior party without the delight of children's art on the walls, or the Orpheus 2000 party without the frisson of funk, even if it was only attempted funk. And the seventh party, the one Tad couldn't remember that morning, he still couldn't remember, but he took that as a sign of skipability.

Instead, he chose the toughest, most dazzling ticket, and seeing Dean. The slightly woozy, sentimental Tad thought facing this dicey situation would be therapeutic and soul-strengthening, like running the gamut, or gauntlet, whatever that was. Chopping down the cherry tree was bad, but setting the record straight might make him presidential.

Besides, the party would be tourist-flatteningly lavish. It was to be at Dean's fifty-year-old boyfriend Kris Van Dusen's penthouse on upper Fifth Avenue. "Doozy" Van Dusen was rich, if not beyond Tad's wildest dreams, then certainly beyond

Tad's practical ability to understand. Doozy always figured on annual top ten richest executive lists—another piquant aspect to Christmas was the year-end lists that amounted to autopsies on the dying year, as if the world was partying on a gigantic dying animal and these were the pertinent stats. Doozy—a nickname his enemies relished even more than his intimates—was one of the few businessmen whose face the general public recognized from the gossip columns, which was the modern equivalent of a niche in the Pantheon. He was bald as a comic-book supervillain, heir to a fortune in food thickeners (Van Dusen ice cream and chocolates stood for quality, if you shopped only at supermarkets), and he had solidified it further by investing in several Hollywood blockbusters, including that year's latest all-time box-office success, *DinoZombies,* whose plot points had dominated playground chatter at Excelsior for months. As his cab pulled up at the corner of Seventy-ninth and Fifth, it occurred to Tad that the CD-ROM DinoZombies game that Nat and Rekha had given Hunter had probably put money in this guy's pocket.

The doorman instantly guessed Tad's destination and waved him ahead. As he rode the elevator up, warm and hopeful, Tad grinned, recalling how he and Nat had always pretended elevators were Molecular Re-Arrangers, and you weren't changing floors—the elevator was stationary, you were merely reconfiguring all the matter outside the door.

The elevator also reminded him of the concentration booths on quiz shows, and, as if cramming for an exam, he riffled through his few memories of Dean, with whom, after all, he'd slept only once. When they'd met, Dean had been beguiled by Tad's high-octane blarney: "Parish as in church zone, or Perish as in die?" Their encounter, which Tad chose to remember as passionate, was actually a struggle for dominance where neither would give way. Almost as compensation rather than consequence, afterward Dean had mouthed words to the effect that it was too bad Tad was already taken, and Tad had not recognized it as the sort of salesman's lie told for credit, like a check that can't be cashed, and he'd brashly thought the experiment's results were reproducible. Dean was already seeing Doozy, it turned out.

The elevator opened with a relieved *whoosh,* as if it had been holding its breath, and Tad stepped into a beautiful black-and-white-tiled foyer that reminded him of *Alice in Wonderland.* The first words he overheard as he entered the apartment, despite a din from the larger rooms beyond, were from one of two tawny young women, presumably fashion models, certainly taller than he, and pneumatically packed into little black dresses and sheer nylons like poison-flavored Popsicles. They wore glittering accessories at their necks and earlobes that reminded Tad early man worshiped gold because the stars, sun, and moon were not accessible, and what little he knew of ecstasy was that it was brilliant and shimmering, and was not night, with its unseen predators and cold.

The women's brownish lipstick was outlined with a darker line, which made them look like errant children caught eating chocolate. One of the variations on blond was finishing a story, and giggled to her virtual twin, "It was so funny! I died! I *literally* died!"

The suggestion of entering the afterlife made tipsy Tad hesitate, but he entered the larger room beyond. Slowly the chic heft of the party began to register. A smoothly unobtrusive party staffer had somehow taken Tad's leather jacket without his even realizing it, like the disembodied hands in the Beast's castle. Candlelight and foil bunting everywhere gave the sheen of sunlight on water, or of torchlight on Ali Baba's treasure—that is, the treasure belonging to others which Ali Baba accidentally discovers. From somewhere drifted a live, light trumpeted jazz version of "Angels We Have Heard on High." Again, Tad thought, *The joyous strain . . .*

He felt like the lost traveler in the enchanted glade, and in his blue jeans he was even more the hunchbacked Celtic yokel who stumbles upon the revels. The setting made him think of Queen Mab's throne room of gossamer turquoise immortals, or Olympus with its pristine linen togas and ambrosia, only here the color of immortality was, paradoxically, black. Everywhere were the short dresses and tieless suits of the posturing "Amerotrash" types Tad was jealous of even when he was in their midst. Even at eighteen and nineteen, the Hale clubbies had worn all black, hoping to simulate the tragedy of actual experience. Hearing their older selves' laughter, Tad uneasily wondered if they'd successfully found tragedy or not. For a moment, he flashed on the nightmare that had awakened him that morning.

The room was electric with the party's desirability. Copies of Dean's magazine, *Vision,* were piled on one table like the journalistic canapés they were. Older but eagle-eyed deal makers mixed with actors and models whom Tad half-recognized from the newspapers, though the gossip columns were so near to nonfiction, he tried to avoid them. He seldom went to the movies, but he imagined this was second- or thirdhand familiarity, like seeing the headline of a review of a film rather than the film itself.

And—there was Dean, not far away, but distant, due to the crowd, glorious and golden as a roast turkey. Botox injections had made his face smooth but rigid and expressionless, the bright red cummerbund of his tuxedo substituting for personal fire. He was nodding his square jaw at another tall, handsome guest—like animals at watering holes, tall and short seem to find their own at cocktail parties—his eyes motionless, at attention. Dean was younger than Tad but seemed older—he was bland before his time, but that's what had attracted Tad. Dean was a house with a leakproof basement. Tad himself was what Realtors try to sell as a fixer-upper.

When Dean scanned the room, as hosts must, he saw Tad,

but his already-stiff face froze in what was clearly unhappy horror. He gave a maitre d'-like closed-eye dismissal to whomever he was talking with and approached Tad as if the overaged waif were festooned with a tunic of land mines. "*What are you doing here?*" he asked Tad in unconcealed fright.

"Dean!" Tad tried to restrain his own response until he understood what was happening. "Thanks for inviting me to your party!" Dean still looked frightened, and didn't compose himself. "I assumed you wanted to let bygones be bygones. Be friends?" Tad elaborated.

Dean's face fell, like a ceiling collapsing onto Tad, in that ingenuous way thoughtless people have of revealing their feelings. "*I didn't invite you!*"

Tad's self-imagined harvest of magnanimity had been overrun by an unforeseen plague of emotionless locusts. Bygones were indeed bygones.

Then a wave of thought washed up on Dean's tanned face's beach. "Ohhhh! You must have been on the mailing list! I had Doozy's assistant do the inviting! You must have given to one of his charities in the last year, or I just didn't cut you from my list. It wasn't intentional, anyhow!"

Tad's fantasies of amazing grace were twisted like a hectic ankle on an unexpected curb. He had meant to appear noble, but here he was being the peasant.

Dean was just starting to realize that his abruptness might not have been the savviest host behavior. "As I said, I never actually crossed you out of my book. And you are arguably nice. I know how interested you are in heaven and all. You probably gave money to one of Doozy's charities. . . . Oh, I said that already. Well, I mean, you're welcome to be here, though. You were invited, just . . . not by a human." The invitation was engraved, not personal.

Tad squirmed, though for whose sake, he couldn't tell. "Well . . . Can you handle it? I won't stay long."

Dean looked at Tad with eyes as still as a blind man's. "No, no! Don't go. In a way, I don't care. I'm just so surprised! You look great!"

Tad, like Bonny and everyone else, tried to go with these unexpected rewrites. Dean wasn't his pining ex, and he wasn't his enemy; he was just a slightly careless guest star on Tad's life's marathon program. Tad responded to the dialogue he heard, at the moment, through a fog, or, rather, through a sudden lack of fog. "No, I don't look great. I'm underdressed for this."

"Well, I think you look fine. But then, I'm *totally* partial!" That was Dean, Tad mused: totally partial. "*Anyway*," Dean resumed, using the word that indicates a conversation's end. "You enjoy! Go upstairs on the terrace! There's a live display up there that you will not believe! You must see it! I have to go say hi to some people from the magazine." Dean had imaginary friends of his own to conjure when required, and he sent problems away rather than handle them, because the rich can.

Tad, alone among shiny bobbing strangers, felt a slight mane of sweat under his now slightly wrinkled white shirt collar, the accumulating wine and the self-consciousness alchemically basting him. A circulating photographer was taking flash pictures with a camera that seemed intentionally bulky for old-style glamour purposes, heightening the feeling that the party was a news event. He made no attempt to photograph Tad.

The question repeated again and again on all sides was, "Are you going away for the holidays?" Most New Yorkers go back to the places they're from at Christmas, one day of community outreach service for the crime of living in New York. Someone near Tad announced, "Just because Cuba has Christmas again doesn't mean I have to go back there!" and another confided to an unseen friend, "But the *third* time I was in Tuscany, I was bored bored bored!"

Privilege seemed ludicrous at that moment, and Tad wondered why he courted it, just as he wondered why he commanded himself to write a needless thesis. He saw that Dean had exactly the same problem he had, only tall, lean Dean had grown up feeling *financially* short. Tad thought of the one long afternoon he'd spent in bed with Dean, over a year before. During one interval in the intentionally darkened room, Dean had reminisced about being a busboy at a hotel in his native Detroit, how angry he used to feel as the automotive power brokers had pastry-and-coffee panels on Action Strategy while their sequinned wives, in outlanders' outlandish ideas of finery, had Fashion Preview lunches in the adjacent ballroom, really two conference rooms with a folding accordion wall removed. Dean was the busboy who wanted to have his own busboys, and here tonight he had them. Dean might have liked Tad as a person, but for his own cannibal objectives, Tad was empty calories. And from Tad's heart's demoralized but idealistic core, Dean was love's junk food, too.

Tad, a mouse at the rat race, a shade among the living, fiscally speaking, took some champagne from a passing Triumphal Foods waiter's tray. Wine would be his stopgap friend, the courtesy car while his future was still being tinkered with at the garage.

To seem like he had something to do, he hovered by a table of what his folklore reading would describe as "choice viands," only they were partly obscured by twining vegetation and fresh flowers, as if the food were in a terrarium resembling its natural habitat. One platter he discerned was of steak tartare, red and glistening, with small serving knives in it to facilitate spreading it on the doll-sized slices of toasted bread offered alongside. The knives studding the raw flesh seemed a strange postmortem reenactment of the matador conquering the bull with his cache of swords. In his mind's idleness and tendency to drift, Tad then pictured the dish as a World War I doughboy entangled in the barbed wire of no-man's-land. He shuddered to realize that above all it resembled the agonizing bright red picture of Christ's thorn-choked sacred heart that had hung in the Silvarinis' living room as they smoked, drank, and laughed beneath it.

The two beautiful women he'd seen when he arrived were now at his shoulder, fishing through the contents of two identical bags, black canvas totes with the Van Dusen Industries logo on them in tastefully small letters.

"Hi!" One grinned when she sensed Tad watching her, and she tried to atone for what she supposed must have looked like girlish greed. "Did you know there's a free tote bag full of stuff for every guest here?"

"Wow!" Tad nervously figured he'd better play along until he could figure out whether to stay or leave the party, which now seemed as noisy as trackside at the Indianapolis 500. He put down his empty champagne flute and picked up someone's abandoned glass of wine off a side table. He took a healthy— or, actually, unhealthy—sip.

"Ooo, are you old enough to drink?" one of the models asked him, not critically, but conspiratorially. She had been drinking and smoking since fourteen.

"I'm forty-five," Tad answered, as if factually.

"Wow, you look great!" the too-trusting sophisticate answered.

"Just so long as you're twenty-one or over!" Her companion teased.

Tad smiled. "Oh, I'm not twenty-one, but I'm *definitely* over!"

They didn't seem to catch his pessimism, but he himself didn't know if he meant it or not. "Do you have a regimen, or is it just some lucky glandular thing?" The first woman asked, like a ready pupil. "I wish I still looked twelve! I'd be getting more lingerie ads!"

The other model tactfully moved the conversation ahead. "Speaking of regimen—there's a certificate here for a massage at Elysium! Isn't that great?" Tad vaguely sensed from the ads in *Vision* that this meant it was a two-hundred-dollar value, and his inner mom disapproved of the self-indulgence but simultaneously whistled at so rarefied freebie.

"Have you ever had a professional massage?" the first one asked him innocently, which a straight man might have hoped was a come-on but which Tad knew was mere chat.

"Well, I've been slapped to my senses a few times." He smiled, thinking of his encounter with Dean a minute earlier.

Both models laughed uproariously. It's easy to forget that models live in a hell of insecurity, and need occasional relief. "I know what you mean!" One laughed. "That is so incredibly credible!"

"I do, too!" the other one said. "My agent sent me out for a housewife part in a cleanser ad last week! That made me think! Like, am I now supposed to be the nice one at home? Do I no longer seem to be the one they leave the nice one at home for?"

"That is a juncture," Tad offered automatically.

"I didn't get the ad. My agent said they said I was too exotic, so I take comfort in that."

One of the young women contemplated the recesses of her gift tote. "Oh, there's excellent chocolate in here, too! I hate that!"

Tad, flushed now and trying to conceal his tipsiness, though with increasing difficulty, edged away from this self-contained panel. He hadn't been this drunk for almost a year, not since last January, on the feast of the Epiphany. It had been his first night alone in Garth's sublet after leaving Angelo, and his bad handling of the separation slowly hit him as he sat and sipped the fine old scotch Les had sent all his male family members and valued clients as holiday connection maintenance.

Tad knew he should leave, but, in his unemployment and unattachment, he felt compelled to guzzle this party like water before, camel-fashion, he entered what might be a vast social desert. Besides, he was in the land of the lotus-eaters, and he felt addicted to its debilitating charms.

He wandered from room to room, some of which had biblically costumed waiters offering trays of hors d'oeuvres, while others featured bodybuilders dressed as sleeveless elves, in short shorts that would have caused hypothermia at the North Pole, tending bar behind white-clothed tables. He peeked into the room where the jazz improvements on the old standards were coming from. *"And heaven and nature sing, switch-a-rooney, and heaven and nature sing . . ."* All these centuries of ecstatic musical composition, Tad thought, all focused on one day. It's Christ's Super Bowl halftime. Tad felt an unaccountable twinge when he saw his downstairs neighbor Roscoe was the trumpet player in the hired trio.

Roscoe and his combo mates wore white tuxedoes, and from their small elevated platform they looked like angels from that old-fashioned modern-dress heaven where swing has replaced harps. They also reminded Tad of Angelo trick-or-treating in his First Communion suit. Tad's impulse was to wave and get his cannibal credit for direct connection to hipness, but Roscoe was either happily or professionally lost down the avenues of melody—he wasn't looking at the guests. Tad didn't approach him, somehow assuming Roscoe would think less of him for being a silly partygoer instead of a poor downtrodden neighbor.

"Tad!" A woman's voice called. He turned, to see Yoni, her radical air and hair concealed under a placid wimple, and in a crisp Virgin Mary blue wraparound cloak.

"Yoni! You're working here!" He overacted his surprise in the noise of the room.

"Hey, this way the outfit gets double duty, here and at my show! Crab cake?" She offered her tray with a droll milkmaid curtsy. "Norman's doing the vegetarian dumplings, see?" She indicated a pocket of space in a far corner, where Norman, in the gold-trimmed purple robes of one of the Magi, and the traditional gilded muffin-shaped hat, was silently holding a tray while a dipsomaniacal couple indifferent to his presence heatedly discussed their personal problems, pointing the toothpicks they'd speared their dumplings with at each other for emphasis.

"Norman got to be one of the three kings because of the goatee tattoo," Yoni confided in the din. "It makes him seem more *from-Orient-are.*" Tad marveled at the idea that here Norman had to hold his tongue while others spoke.

"Whoa," Tad announced to no one in particular. "The Venn diagrams are starting to overlap!"

"What?" Yoni asked. Her trove of arcana didn't include math.

"I know more of the employees here than I know guests," he recited slowly, as if some object lesson had just been visited upon him.

"Well, it's not surprising. Have you been up on the roof?" Yoni asked unexpectedly, her eyes unusually wide for a middle-aged woman.

"No, but Dean says there's a display—"

"Tad Leary, you cosmic man-boy you! It's amazing! They had a rink *installed* for this party! You must see it!"

Nearby, the photographer called to Yoni. "Hey, Blessed Virgin Mary! How about a photo op with you and these gals?" The two functionally blond women were giggling next to him.

Yoni looked more pleased than put-upon, but she murmured to Tad, "Noblesse oblige!" She put down her tray briefly to position her pastel robe between the black-sheathed models, who kicked up a heel each and bussed the Queen of Heaven on her cheek in playful obeisance.

"Good, good!" the photographer called. "Better yet—now let's get Mary between those bodybuilders! The BVM with the BVDs!" Angelo's brothers loved cheesecake and even porno, and they would have vocally encouraged the two models to undress, but the women's fully dressed sporting with the image of the Virgin would have scandalized them.

Tad left Yoni to her combination of servitude and beatification, and deliberately climbed the carpeted stairs to the penthouse terrace to see the spectacle whose coming had been foretold to him. What was ordinarily a vast patio space had been partially converted to a small ice-skating rink, and on it a young couple in rococo tights were demonstrating accomplished ice-dancing routines. Tad thought of the nightclubs in old movies, where the patrons ate and drank while a dance team performed inches away. The wind at the rooftop's height was very cold, so only a few spectators braved it to watch the sideshow, though Tad recognized the couple as recent Olympic-medalist skaters. As a child, he'd thought hiring a magician for a birthday party was the apex of visible expense. But then, he'd thought freestanding frame pools were unattainably deluxe.

As he watched the pair glide in necessarily constricted circles, wondering whether they were married, and how they could leap through the air and risk breaking their necks together day after day, year after year, Tad heard a cow moo. Behind him was another display, a tiny fenced-in petting zoo of farm animals attended by two men dressed as New Testament shepherds. They dispensed the hay, and Tad momentarily wondered if they were part of the Triumphal Foods staff. Had there been any children at the party, this would have been its epicenter, with its sheep, goats, and cow for those ordinarily powerless little people to condescend to. Poultry somehow have never had the status or warmth to figure in crèche tableaux.

Tad, though he was shivering in just his shirt, dutifully circled the pen and patted each animal's head. Since he seemed to know the staff better than the celebrities, he pretended to know the barnyard animals personally, as well. "Hi, Carla," he greeted the cow. "See ya back at the barn!" He gave the sheep the thumbs-up sign. "Hi, Hughie, hi Skip! At least *you've* got a job!" He zapped the goat with the salutory index finger of the cocktail phony. "Billy, you still got that goat thing goin'!"

One of the temp shepherds, whose lit cigarette under-mined his costume's antique effect, eyed Tad dubiously, so Tad felt he should say something demonstrably normal. "How did you get them all up here?" he asked.

"Service elevator," the shepherd answered indifferently.

Tad could muster no other questions, so he squinted at the man approvingly and ambled back inside and downstairs. He again caromed from room to room, but there was no chink in any clique for him to insert himself. He mused that he could probably hide behind the drapes and live in Doozy's expansive place for years, undiscovered as a mouse, but, of course, Dean wouldn't like the discovery that he was, in fact, living with Tad, albeit unwittingly.

In the far room, Roscoe's combo was playing a bluesy take on " I Wonder as I Wander." Finally, Dean, to paint over his rejection of Tad, sought him out again. Only a few minutes had passed, but to a guest who knows no one, a few minutes can seem like an hour.

"Come meet Doozy!" he said, "if he isn't *already* mobbed by people with ideas for projects!" The word *already* sounded strange to Tad, as if he, Tad, had an idea for a project. There was his *Social Hierarchies of Imaginary Places,* but it didn't feel like a real project anymore, at least not tonight.

Dean led him to the main room and introduced him to several well-tonsured guests, but Tad, to his inner alarm, found he was starting to have trouble understanding anything that was being said. What he heard was, "Tad, this is Brandish Alba-core. He's a lawyer at Hector, Harris and Hound. And this is Jitney Spires. He's a trader at Sachs and Sachs."

"Sacks and sacks, that's straightforward. You're mighty *mighty.*" Tad had turned off his inner censor. Half-jealous, half-dismissive, he concluded this was a crowd to whom Christmas meant, above all, *bonus!* Dean and the two men were speaking, but he hardly heard them over the sizzling of his mental stove. Somebody used the word *Congress,* or possibly it was *Commerce,* and Tad asked himself if at this level there was really any difference between the two.

"Brandish, Jitney—Tad is the most eligible bachelor in New York!"

The desperate undertow of this glistening wave of a compliment disturbed Tad. "Not the most," he added politely. "Just the best."

"That's the attitude!" one of them said with the jauntiness required at business institutions, but in a minute they had both wandered to more familiar faces, leaving Tad free to tour the halls like a documentarist without a camera. He again tasted a strange remorse for his small-minded rejection of unimpressive but genuinely encouraging Angelo.

"There he is!" Dean approached Tad urgently, as if he'd just sighted a famous man he didn't know personally, and grabbed Tad's arm to lead him to the presence of Doozy. Whereas everyone else was wearing fanciful black evening clothes, Kris Van Dusen stuck to his daytime business suit. His bulletlike shaved head turned the supposed liability of baldness into an aggressive gesture—with Norman, it seemed like desperate guesswork—and combined with the fact he was short, though taller than Tad, he seemed to radiate potential energy like a compact and polished nuclear warhead.

He was explaining an upcoming project to the two models in black Tad had met earlier. "The working title is *Mall Zombies.* 'Shop *after* you drop!'"

"Tad Leary, Kris Van Dusen! Kris, my friend Tad!" Dean said hurriedly, as if Tad had now seen the big local attraction and could leave. The hovering lady models apparently didn't need to be introduced.

Doozy's piercing gaze would have made Tad want to fold his poker hand had he had one. "So, you know my *current* boyfriend," Doozy said tartly. He and Dean had lived together for almost a year, but Tad wondered if he was joking or pragmatic.

"Just barely!" Tad answered, which was supposed to minimize his guilt about how he knew Dean, but it made the situation even wobblier.

"Tad does . . ." Dean began, then paused, and Tad could sense that Dean was at a loss for verbs where he was concerned. "Um . . . Oh! Are you still doing that angels and devils thing, that, like, baseball program, like which ones are the generals and which are the sergeants and, uh . . . pawns?"

"Yes!" Tad tried to explain, though he was surprised to find words began to elude him. The wine was rushing past his temples. "Yes, absolutely! Lucifer, Satan, Mephistopheles, Beelzebub, Nicodemus . . . Sometimes they're all the same being and sometimes they're distinct from each other."

Doozy gave a disinterested stare, as if he were at a pitch meeting for a movie he wasn't likely to fund. "I assumed they were all one man with a lot of aliases." To Doozy, Satan was just another competitor.

"No, some of them were gods who got discredited when Christianity came in. Baal, Moloch. All those guys."

The octopedal businessman processed the information, even while spreading some cheese on a cracker and surveying the room for more sober and less superfluous company. "Oh, blame the previous administration, huh?"

"Well, like . . . they took Egypt's Set and made him Satan."

"That sounds like some maxim from the *Farmer's Almanac*," Doozy said distractedly, since he was thinking about several other things simultaneously.

The two good-natured models, who'd stood by mutely, now ventured into the conversation like student drivers edging into speeding traffic. "My big question is," one of them jumped in, and paused for emphasis. "Who *designed* hell? God? The devil? I mean, is that how He *wants* it? Those stone things that hang from the ceiling? Don't get me wrong, I'm not saying I don't *like* it."

"It looks like a club."

"Yeah. Heaven, though, is too brightly lit."

"Yes, not flattering."

Doozy was looking at someone on the other side of the room but phoned in his side of the conversation. "Well, if you're noncorporeal, how unflattering can light be?"

Dean conscientiously tried to return to normality insofar as he grasped it. "Mmm! Patina—is that Jamais you're wearing?"

"Yes!" One of the women beamed. "Men usually don't recognize fragrances!"

Dean smiled bashfully, deft at gradations of glamour. "Well, remember, *Vision* did that promotional party for them after they bought four successive back covers."

"Yes, but all my friends confuse it with Significance."

This talk seemed bizarre to Tad, and it made him recall a childhood game, when he, Nat and Les would sit on the steps to play "Cars." It was a game that status-seeker Les had devised. They'd sit on the front porch steps and wait for autos to pass in the street, and whichever one passed on your turn was your car. The fanciest car won. Tad had never much liked the game, because all cars looked basically the same to him, and Les's delight in getting a Saab over Nat's Ford and Tad's Dodge was lost on him.

Doozy changed the subject by announcing to the models, whom he apparently knew, "Dean and I are going to Saint Bart's for the holidays." Tad mentally commented to himself that Saint Bart must be the patron saint of luxury, though another side of him punctiliously reported that Bartholomew was one of the apostles, flayed by disbelievers and so he had become the patron saint of tanners and skin handlers, though you'd think he would have been against them rather than in favor of them. Tad was losing his concentration on the party as prevailing reality.

"Mmm!" One of the models nodded her approval. "We all had so much fun together down in Presto Largo last year!" Tad was intrigued and confused until she added, "It was such a relief to get away from sex for a while!"

Disoriented, Tad responded, with a touch too much vehemence, "I just don't see how you can voluntarily go someplace hot for Christmas!"

Doozy breezily countered, "Well, Jesus chose to, didn't He? The Middle East, after all."

There was an awkward pause, and for some reason Tad remembered his crisis. "*I need a job!*" he blurted.

Dean looked surprised and hurt, as if he never would have guessed that Tad really was one of those many people with a project, who suffocatingly hurled themselves at Doozy like dung beetles at an elephant spoor.

"Do you do anything in the real world?" Doozy asked evenly, the way you back out of the room and don't raise your voice when you meet a madman.

"I'm good with children," Tad gurgled, aware his lightweight resumé would blow off any desk. "Maybe I could deal with movie executives. . . ."

That was an old joke to Doozy, but he let it pass. "Do you keep books?"

Tad misunderstood him, thinking in his superannuated student way of lending and borrowing textbooks. Simon, it flashed across his mind, still had his copy of *The Dictionary of Phantoms*. "No, I always return them," he said with pride, though Doozy maintained his neutral expression, unsure if Tad had made an intentional joke this time or not.

Doozy was abruptly and literally buttonholed by another ambitious guest and playfully dragged by the necktie to another corner of the room. Dean and the models followed, or used the moment as an excuse to disperse, anyway. Tad felt he had socially soiled himself.

The party wheels ground, moving the guests on tiny tracks

from one clot of company to another. Tad blew his nose in a paper napkin decorated with reindeer dancing on their hind legs, but he felt it was wrong, somehow, as if he should have gone to one of the bathrooms and found plain white tissue whose job description it was to service noses. Then he didn't know where to put it, since there were no wastebaskets in sight. It would be clumsy to give its wet wad to one of the caterers, so he found an abandoned plate, or at least he hoped it was, and left it alongside the crumbs and toothpicks.

After Tad eased away from the scene of his crime, he found himself standing by a tall dark-haired man who rakishly wore a toothbrush in his blazer lapel. The man grinned in anticipatory triumph, as if Spin the Bottle had just brought the two together. His graven handsomeness made Tad avert his eyes, as from sun on snow. It seemed insulting, somehow, like a stranger's boom box playing in your ear.

"Hey, baby!" he sang, as if used to daily conquest. Ordinarily, lovers of all sizes call each other "baby," but it alienated Tad. "Do you like what you see?"

His self-assurance annoyed Tad, whom the alcohol was starting to depress. "I don't know," he answered without inflection. "You're standing in my line of vision."

This unknown man must have been getting bleary himself, because he didn't seem to register what Tad had said. "Are you a stylist, too?"

"Oh, I don't know," Tad said, playacting a drunken philosopher even though he actually was one. "I guess we're all stylists, just trying to apply creme rinse and a comb to our tangled lives."

This pleased his tall companion, who gasped as if balloons had just fallen from the ceiling. "Yes! Yes! And Doozy is a money stylist! He takes flat bank accounts and makes them all fluffy and shiny!" Tad had no idea if this image was apt. The only financial scheme he'd ever undertaken was when he made a self-concerted effort to spend all of the jarful of stray nickels and dimes he had accumulated at Garth's. As Tad ordinated the kingdom of coins, dimes and nickels were the Lesser Silvers.

The leonine stylist put his hand on Tad's shoulder and gripped it, a presumption Tad recognized as the first step of a bully's forced seduction. Battery as flattery.

"So, are you in a relationship?" he asked. Tad didn't even know this beefcake hot dog's name.

"No, I'm not." Tad resumed the witness-box leadenness a sober man would have recognized as a brush-off. Now he chided himself for making no effort earlier with the lawyer and banker, who at least were well-mannered.

"Not even a long-distance one?"

"If I have one, it's so long-distance I have no idea who he is."

The stylist took this as encouragement. "I'm Jack. Like the guy in the deck of cards."

"Ah!" Tad had never liked the supercilious jack in the deck of cards. It was untrustworthy and unaccountable, an interloper between the rational ascending numbers and the higher queen and king. The ace, presumably, was God, the oneness greater than manyness, but who was Jack? The queen's gigolo?

"I should warn you—I have multiple personalities! It's called multiple personality disorder! Right now, I'm Jack the Jock, but sometimes I'm Kooky Jack, or Hungry Jack. When I'm asleep, I call myself Sleeping Jack. That is, when I'm awake, that's what I call myself when I'm asleep. So that's four personalities right there. I'm an adventure!"

"If I had to guess, I'd say you had single personality deficiency," the mad side of Tad spoke.

"No, it's called something else. But it means, I can be wild!" Again, the stranger gripping his shoulder didn't seem to understand. In a way, Tad relished treating a tall man rudely, but it was like boxing someone drugged. In his disinhibited inebriation, Jack the Stylist—though whether of faces, food, or cabaret song, Tad didn't know—thought he was flirting by proceeding to ask Tad, "Have you ever had your asshole shaved?"

Tad put an *X* through his vision of the man, pointedly removed the hand from his shoulder, and managed to answer, "No." He now used the monosyllabic approach favored on airplane flights with unwelcome chatty seatmates.

Jack continued. "I did once. At a party."

Tad wobbled in bewilderment, and lost control of his monotone. "You mean, you not only did it, it was . . . *witnessed?*"

His suitor seemed to retract his suit, since Tad was evidently prudish, or proving uncooperative, anyway. "It wasn't a Christmas party," he explained defensively. Tad thought of the family joke—*Imagine my surprise to encounter a frictionless surface.*

The frictionless beauty wandered off, seeking a frailer antelope, and without wasting his resources further by bothering to excuse himself from Tad's company. The party gears accordingly turned, bringing Doozy back to Tad's side. Unnervingly for a titan of industry, Doozy remarked of the retreating stylist, "Well. He's got the bod of God!"

Tad was no longer interested in or capable of dutiful conversation, and he simply spoke his thoughts as he whimsically pursued the point. "God the Father, or God the Son? Burly Jehovah or skinny sacrifice? God the Holy Ghost doesn't even have a body, exactly. . . . Well, that bird-act thing . . . I always wanted it to be an actual ghost, you know, full-length ectoplasm and with holes for eyes. . . ."

Doozy stared. "I was thinking along Apollo lines." Evidently, Doozy's god was pagan.

Again, there was the tense silence that grips ordinary folk trapped with the famous. "Maybe you could hire me as a stealth bodyguard!" Tad improvised, trying to make light of his earlier importunism. "They wouldn't see me until it was too late!"

"That's funny," Doozy said without smiling. As he'd sell

a tumbling stock, he then decided Tad was unprofitable, and gravitated to another cluster of guests. Tad accepted the rejection painlessly as alcohol's anesthetic started to embalm him. He wandered along one of the halls, away from the party's pulsing downtown and upstairs to a peaceful suburban end of the penthouse.

In a small library of leather-bound, never-disturbed volumes, and what looked like Masonic decorations—Tad didn't know for sure—alcohol-mellowed Dean was sitting in an armchair, taking a break from what were primarily Doozy's associates with a gin and tonic in solitude. He seemed to be contemplating the unpredictably winking light patterns on a small but professionally decorated tabletop tree, as if he were trying to crack their Morse code for a secret message. Even the ice in his drink tinkled significantly, like a secret consortium whispering an explanation in a language Tad didn't speak.

Dean held up his drink. "It takes at least two ice cubes to make a gracious drink," he declared, either theorizing or reciting. "One is inadequate." He indicated the momentarily unattended caterer's bar nearby and said, "Tad! Join me for a nightcap!" He seemed ready to play out a heart-to-heart politely with Tad, and Tad complied, partly because this was the scenario he'd idealized, and partly because it would be awkward to decline this invitation to what would probably be his last conversation with a man who had, after all, rejected him.

Dean poured two scotches, neat. It saved time. "Sorry about everything again," he said as they clinked glasses. "I only said I wished I was with you to be nice, you know, to encourage you. I thought you would stay with that little Italian guy."

"No, no, I was reckless," Tad said, tumbling into the moment of reconciliation he thought he'd come there for, and realizing that, in fact, it had been his own fault for believing Dean's compliments without any collateral to make them credible. The scotch scalded his tongue, and then soothed it.

"And, I know this sounds crazy," Dean, a little drunk himself, revealed, "but for some reason, I was just too weirded out by that double-jointed thumb of yours. When you stretched it back that way, *brr!* It was just too unusual for me."

Tad embraced this superficial answer as more likely to be true than any other. "It's what had to happen," he blathered. "I stupidly thought my happiness was somewhere else, not . . ." He didn't finish his sentence—his train of thought had derailed—but Dean didn't seem to mind.

"What was the happiest you ever were?" Dean eventually asked, to mend the torn conversation, proud of the question's profundity.

Tad thought he shouldn't mention Angelo, though why he was still so careful about Dean's feelings, he couldn't say. "I guess when I played Puck in college."

"You played hockey? Are you big enough?"

"Puck, the head elf in *A Midsummer Night's Dream*."

"Oh, right, I saw the dance version. But . . . Puck is a *servant*."

"Well, but the part is powerful. He is magical, and the audience is in his hands. He controls the onstage humans, too. He's immortal and having a great time."

Dean seemed satisfied by this, since it was cordiality and not genuine curiosity that had prompted him. "I had a frightening glimpse of my own mortality this morning," he confided to Tad. "I was getting my hair cut for the party, and the barber offered to trim my eyebrows. 'Trim your eyebrows, sir?' *Brrr!* That has never happened to me before." He looked into the fire, itself starting to sputter. "And I thought nostril hair was adulthood's worst thing. You don't have to worry about that, though, do you? Your little body's as hairless as a schoolboy's!" This unintentionally irked Tad, but annoyance at a lost love can be a distinct blessing.

Dean, clearly unused to confessionalism, seemed to relish this opportunity. "Here, come with me in here. These are my private rooms, Doozy let me do them however I wanted!" One wall of the library swung around like a secret entrance in a haunted house, but in his floating intoxication Tad took the novelty quite matter-of-factly. "There's another way in, but this is the fun way." It seemed as if showing Tad this room was a gesture of intimacy.

The room was a sleek, highly modern study with black furniture and appliances, and he and Tad sat in two adjacent luscious black leather executive swivel chairs. Tad was hardly registering the room itself, focusing instead on making sense of Dean's off-putting friendliness.

"I have to tell you," Dean said, "how much I admire how you've chosen a life of poverty and obscurity, doing something that can never pay off!"

It was supposed to be a compliment. Tad again remembered Dean's postcoital bitter monologue about working at that Detroit hotel, whereas Angelo had never had any qualms about his blue-collar identity, and at least Angelo had some grasp of what Tad's graduate studies were about. Dean was all wrong for him. The crisp quality that had seemed so ideal and healthy now seemed to be almost perverse. He was highfalutin' and anal-retentive, unlike low-falutin', sloppy, all-embracing Angelo.

The room's appliances, TV console, and even toilet had been specially designed to be hidden from the eye by cabinets as black as jet, as they say in the fairy tales, in order to simulate a world where elegant people aren't required to shit, eat, or even move. Somehow, even Dean's senatorial speech was like he'd practiced and scrubbed his voice clean, just as Tad had done. Dean had a WASPy name, but he was from anonymous generations of subsistence farmers. They were the same person, Tad now understood, except Tad didn't need a king, he just wanted a kingdom. Dean had found his prince, though, or, anyway, his palace, in Doozy's penthouse, where Doozy's only demand was a lover who never made a scene. Dean loved the heights, since he had no fear of heights, just a fear of depth. Shallow be thy name.

Still, Dean, like Minus, seemed to have risen effortlessly to security, whereas Tad was going to have to fight for the foreseeable future just for shelter. His head churned like an overloaded washing machine that lacked for fabric softener, and he went back through the revolving wall into the library, thanking Dean hastily and pleading the need to go home, unaware how real that need was. The clock began to strike midnight, the only moment of the day, besides noon, significant enough to have its own name. There, suddenly incarnate, standing ready to serve at the white-tableclothed bar, was his folklore nemesis, Simon.

Apparently he, too, was working for the caterers, since he had just carried in a tray of unidentifiable pâté and wore a red elf costume and pointed cap, though, with his saturnine features, he looked more like Old Scratch without his fiddle. Tad defensively stood upright, but his small size made the gesture as unavailing as a jerboa rearing up to resist a large desert snake. In his murky state of mind, he tried to summon up the instructions his grandmother had given him were he ever to encounter a ghost or demon. *"Return from whence you came!"* he was supposed to say, but the charm eluded him.

"Well, well! *Venite, Ignoramus!*" It was another of Simon's indecipherable zingers.

"Simon! Uhhh . . . fancy seeing you here!" Tad barely managed in his surprise and disorientation, knowing the cliché was a mere checkers move compared to Simon's three-dimensional verbal chess games. Simon had a book deal—why should he be taking catering jobs?

"Well, you're about twenty thousand leagues out of your league!" Simon knew how to hit Tad's fear of social inadequacy. "Look at you! My, how the lowly have fallen!"

Tad's responses were slowing. He really hadn't eaten all day, and the mixed drinks were boggling him. "You mean 'lo how the mighty,' don't you?"

"I said what I meant. You don't even get a simple joke?"

Tad was going to counter that at least he was an invited guest, not a flunky, but in the context, it seemed too childishly petty and absurd a point to make, so instead he just stood there. "You're being dandled on the lap of Bacchus," Simon continued, "and you just may fall off, so be careful!" Nothing's worse than when your enemy is absolutely right.

Tad mumbled the obvious. "You're working here? Why, with your Academy Awards and everything?"

Simon gave Tad an ocular tsk-tsk, then said, "There are a lot of important people at this party. I'm not sure you're in any condition to recognize any of them, much less chat them up productively."

Tad wanted to defend himself, and especially to decry the idea that parties were for professional advancement, but he was wrong, and besides, all he could summon was an involuntary fart, which sounded like a duckling or a confused lamb were hidden nearby. Simon laughed, a laugh of triumph Tad thought existed only in old movies, and all tottering Tad could do was concede the field and retreat.

"Good-bye, Mr. Chips!" Simon called after him, which further bewildered Tad, because he knew it was supposed to hurt his feelings, but it sounded harmless. Again, Simon's insults required graduate study. To escape from further inquisition, he stumbled down the stairs to the apartment's main floor and looked for an unoccupied room.

He wandered down a hall and into what was apparently another library, though here, too, was a fully equipped bar and bartender. Candlelight made the library idyllic to Tad, for whom books were escape. Then he saw that the bartender, who was standing at ease but not slouching, even though there were no guests in the room, was Gabe, his faun of the afternoon, dressed not as an angel but as one of the shepherds, with a white burnoose and striped robe.

"Gabe! I'm so happy to see you!"

Gabe was surprisingly unsurprised. Candlelight makes the improbable seem predestined. "Hi! I told you I had to work at a party tonight." He didn't speak Tad's name, and Tad wished he would. He wondered if Gabe remembered it.

"What a wonderful confluence!" Tad said, though his speech was beginning to slur. "But you're Gabriel! You should be dressed as one of the angels!"

"Thanks, but again, I'm just Gabe. Anyway, my supervisor didn't think I was angel material. My complexion is a little too much of this earth."

"Ooh, an evil *pulchritocracy*!" Tad was delighted to make up a word on the spot, but his enunciation kept Gabe from understanding it.

"What? You're a little drunk, my friend."

"I'm winding up my whoopee, and I wasn't expecting to see you! Gee, it's good to see you!" Tad unsteadily touched Gabe's shoulder, but his timing was off, and Gabe stepped back.

"I'm working, Tad," he said simply.

"Tending your sheep." Tad tried to appear supportive. "Where's your staff?"

"My staff? I *am* staff."

"I mean your crook!" Tad sensed he was bowling a gutter ball. "Never mind, never mind!" He tried another tack, but was no luckier. "You know what you can tell me? In 'The First Noël,' when they say it was 'to certain poor shepherds in fields as they lay,' does it mean to some *specific* shepherds, or to *reassure* the shepherds who were there?"

"What are you talking about? Why are you acting like this? You were so nice this afternoon."

"I'm playing an idiot in an upcoming film, and I thought I'd do some Method acting."

"You are the strangest man, and I mean that in *The Guinness Book of Records* sense."

Tad realized he was making a bad third impression. "I want to be normal, I do! Normal normal normal . . . Your love can make me normal!"

"What? I can hardly understand you!"

"Look, I have to be absolutely honest with you," Tad said, slurring, "'cause I want you to trust me!" He made what seemed a serious announcement to him. "I . . . have a double-jointed thumb. I hope that doesn't frighten you!" He pulled his thumb backward as if demonstrating a light switch for the new tenants.

Gabe seemed unfazed. "So? That's pretty cool. I'll bet kids like it." He was right. The kids at Excelsior frequently requested it, just as they loved the father who visited occasionally who could make his eyes vibrate. "That's the least of your problems."

"Thanks!" Tad gushed without comprehension, then resorted to the autopsy-plain truth that drunks think will be helpful. "Oh, Gabe . . . I hope it can work out between us. I want to take care of you."

"Thanks! Huh! . . . I don't really need to be taken care of." Gabe smiled, but he looked uneasily to the doorway, where the two giggling models passed, rummaging in their gift bags to see if they'd missed anything. "I could use some *company* sometimes. But this is not the time to figure that out. And right now, I think you need to take care of yourself."

"Good! I mean, you're right! Well, you know what I mean. But I don't even know if you're older or younger than me!"

"Please! Does that matter to you?"

"Or what you like to do . . ."

Gabe's perpetually furrowed brow deepened its furrow. "Let's not start putting hats on a snowman that isn't built yet."

Tad was no longer monitoring his own speech. "An' so there's no confusion later, um, you should know, I'm a top."

Gabe shuddered. "That is too much information," he

complained. "Can't you get beyond notions like *top* or *bottom* and consider the concept of *partners?*"

"Yes, of course. I didn't mean to presume." Tad now could feel that all that liquid refreshment was the opposite of freshening—it was making him lose control. He was that misleading-sounding adjective *crapulous.* The way heavy rain makes a paper bag likelier to rend, scattering its contents to the sidewalk, his mind was spilling, and he decided he'd better leave before making a scene, especially with Gabe, whose respect he wanted. He was just thankful he hadn't spoken out loud his thought that, in some circumstances, Gabriel is a woman.

Tad pretended to struggle as he pulled his crammed wallet from his pants and pressed it into Gabe's confused hands.

"To show my devotion, let me give you this! It's not literally my heart, but . . . it's the same size, shape, and weight as the heart, and when you wear a jacket, it's right where your heart would be, or is, I mean. And in this wicked ol' city, it's just as crucial an organ as the heart! It's as suicidal as pulling out your heart!"

"I don't think suicidal gestures are seductive," Gabe responded. "I'm a recovering alcoholic myself. I'm not into emergency-rescue jobs. Now take this back, you need it."

In his drunkenness, though, Tad imagined he couldn't retract his noble gesture, and to complete the scene, he quickly and bashfully slipped out of the room.

"Good-bye for now! My heart is yours, though I will need it back eventually!" He had the idea in his head he was the swashbuckler about to climb back down the trellis from his beloved's balcony.

"Tad!" Gabe called after him. Tad heard concern in Gabe's voice, but in his haze, he was gratified that Gabe did indeed remember his name.

Halfway down the hall, Tad regretted his misty improvisation, but to go back now and retract it would compound the image of vacillation and therefore mental instability he had projected. Besides, he'd made a scene with several of the other guests—his inner Donald Duck had escaped—so he decided it really was time to go, and avoiding eye contact with anyone, he hurried through the sparkling oblivious rooms to the elevator. He rushed past the two emblonded models, and though he didn't slow his pace or say good night, he overheard one say to the other, "Ohhh! I am so tired. I have been up *all day!*"

In his mortification and velocity, Tad didn't even reclaim his leather jacket from the coat check, and didn't pick up his gift tote bag, with its free massage certificate, Van Dusen chocolates, DinoZombie CD-ROM, bottle of Jamais, and additional complimentary copy of *Vision*.

"You're nothing but a pack of cards!" he muttered out loud but alone as he stood in the black-and-white-tiled *Alice in Wonderland* foyer. He felt dizzy, and put his outstretched palms on the wall. He had been up all day. He was in the vestibule of the abyss. The elevator opened like the whale mouth for Jonah, and down he rode, if not hell-bound, then at least in that direction. Dash away, dash away, dash away all.

7. A Lovely Empty Glass

In the reality of the street, Tad was angry with himself for leaving his wallet and his jacket at the party, but he didn't dare return, after the scene he imagined he'd made. At least he still had his keys. He'd have to walk home across Central Park. Because of the alcohol, he didn't yet feel the cold. A walk without your wallet is an existential exercise to remind you of life's constant expenses.

The snow had stopped falling and lay in deep drifts: anesthetic, icy sleeping powders on the landscape. It was too wintry and forsaken to need to worry about muggers in the park, and the stars above were crystal clear, an eclipselike rarity in the sky of Manhattan, usually obscured by pollution, reflected glare, and self-absorption. It was as if the dirty air had frozen and fallen to the ground. Tad contemplated the randomly scattered stars, and briefly pitied the ancients for trying to organize them into animals and objects that any child can tell you aren't actually there. With the solstice, he remembered, it was supposed to be the longest night of the year, but somehow in his delirium that was another reason he should walk across the park.

He saw several parked limousines, presumably waiting for Doozy's guests. They reminded Tad of an early childhood round of the "Cars" game he'd played with his brothers. A long black car had passed when it was his turn, so Tad excitedly presumed this limousine would assure him victory. Les and Nat had laughed and informed him that it was a hearse.

Passing the limos, Tad went around the northern end of the Metropolitan Museum to enter the park. It struck him after he'd passed it that he'd gone around it widdershins, to the left, which, according to his grandmother, would decree his doom. Then, even in his grogginess, he rationalized that the Met was a temple of art but not an actual church, so he reassured himself that he should be all right.

Unfortunately, park maintenance workers had built temporary fences blocking the clear-cut path across the softball fields that Tad would have followed instinctively, so he veered off in the nearest available direction, since all the pathways were hidden under the snow's amnesia. The park was uninhabited and turned to wilderness by virtue of midnight and the difficulty of walking. The deep snow made him feel like Frankenstein's monster, forced to take arduous slow steps. Instead of the usual black earth and white sky, the earth was white and the sky was black. The world seemed tipped upside down. What a day he'd had—from uptown, midtown, downtown, uptown, downtown, uptown, and now, crosstown. At least he hoped he was heading crosstown.

Gradually, and with joyless surprise, almost impassively, Tad realized that he had lost his sense of direction. His hobbled consciousness, the drifts that erased all corners, and the darkness all rendered his accustomed visual landmarks obscure. As if to compensate, he tried to run, which was difficult with his hands in his pockets. He fell, and when he used his hands to break the fall, he bloodied them on a rock the snow concealed. He cursed himself for leaving his stocking cap and gloves at Garth's, and, worse, his leather jacket was hanging on a numbered polished-wood hanger back at Dean and Doozy's. The red on his raw palms reminded him for some reason of Christmas red, that holly berries are supposed to be Christ's blood, life despite the midwinter snow. *Because before Easter Lent comes!* In the strangeness of the moment, he seemed to remember Nat telling him that an injured chimpanzee, especially a bloodied one, will be rejected by its fellows. He hastily washed the blood off with snow, but it made his hands ache.

He felt tired, and numb, and the park and the night seemed to extend infinitely in all directions. He also needed to urinate—he'd been drinking for several hours—and he wished he'd interrupted his exit trajectory from Doozy's long enough to relieve himself in the civilized manner, in a secret chamber. Now he paused to pee, as is traditional, against a tree, unobserved, if not in secret, and he marveled as dramatic wholesome-looking steam rose from his unstemmable flowing urine in the icy night air.

I am that merry wanderer of the night! He didn't want to be in this situation a minute longer. His frame lurched, then he felt the ground tilting. After a moment, he sensed that he'd fallen into a snowbank, and, like danger lightly acknowledged in a dream, he dispassionately remarked to himself how ironic it would be if he were to die in a desolate spot in the most crowded place on earth. *Shop, slip, sleep, stop.*

It would be easier not to get up. He remembered playing freeze tag as a child, where tagged players remained frozen until a friend tagged them again to undo the "spell." He didn't like being unfrozen—it was easier to stand still than to race around swatting others and being swatted in return. *Trapped in a world he didn't choose!* He preferred the pit stop. Tad thought of the doomed pig and chicken serving themselves up in the deli earlier. *Embrace your destiny.*

He had never considered suicide in his life, but the alcohol made him dangerously sentimental and dangerously detached simultaneously. So, to his surprise, he thought it over, a big decision like buying a car. Or the farm. Didn't the smart people all give up in those Gunnar Sternland movies? Hadn't Dad apparently given up? Hadn't Les *tried* to give up? Didn't Norman *deserve* to give up?

Another thing that struck him funny as his consciousness wavered was that he was truly his father's son, and he'd beat the old'un into the Alcoholics' Hall of Fatalities. Death would be the ultimate getting drunk, the merciful knockout after a humiliating thirty-four-year sparring match. *Fast away the whole year passes,* as Angelo used to sing incorrectly, but inadvertently correctly, too.

Death is like Christmas, Tad reasoned to himself as he faded. All the hubbub and hysteria in anticipating it, and when the day itself arrives, it's enfolded in silence, a thickly cushioned anticlimax. Israfil's apocalyptic horn is silent, or so high-pitched, the damned don't hear a thing.

Tad reviewed the receding donnybrook—no more rent and tooth decay, no jury duty or laundry or awards shows or having both to read and hear weekly reports of movie box-office receipts. No more phony pro wrestling and real mass murder. No more narcissistic rap, no more antler-clashing ritual display and combat of any kind, no sense of size, but at last, instead, sizelessness. No more hypocrisy, no massive medical-insurance fraud, no labyrinthine personal-insurance forms, no voice mail or phone menus. No more idiots who believe in angels and UFOS but have never marveled at jellyfish and platypi, no more making your name or wiping your ass, no more Midgard, with its oppressive encircling serpent, period. And no more worrying about dying once you're dead—that was tidy. If it's already broke, you don't have to worry about it breaking.

As Tad was relaxing into this permanent vacation, he opened his eyes, almost always a smart move, and recognized the shape of one of the tree boughs over his head. He remembered how he'd bicycled past this spot so many times in recent

summers, part of the weekend consensus of pleasure there—
the strolling lovers or friends, the jogging young mothers
pushing aerodynamic strollers, the teen Roller-bladers both
skilled and scared, the dogs, the occasional wheelchair, and the
other bicyclists, helmeted or windswept—a visual choir, all
flowing southward, down through the unending cathedral
arches of tree branches, with the late-afternoon sunlight coloring the western clouds like layers of a parfait, or else the noon
sun conferring itself exponentially on the boat lake's surface,
from a button to a mesh blanket of brilliance. These were
among the few times Tad wasn't preoccupied with himself, and
communed, owing to the exigencies of heavy one-way traffic,
with the literal river of humanity there. A corpuscle subsumed
in a bloodstream isn't dwelling on its future happiness.

He wanted to ride that route at least once more. Besides,
he was too young to die, he reminded himself. He'd eaten less
than half of his Threescore & Ten candy bar. Certainly his
mother would think his passing was premature. She'd see this as
Infant Crib Death in the four hundred and tenth month.

How absurd it would be to be found frozen, what a humiliation, like Frank the Crank, the village idiot of Dad's abject
childhood mythology, who literally was too stupid to come in
out of the rain and so died of pneumonia. It would make a
ridiculous obituary that would shame Mom and make Simon
laugh, and that was too much. The freezing cold was comfortable, somehow, but he thought of how as a boy he'd sub-
merged himself in the tub one hot summer night and let the
cold water run. It was idyllic, lying hidden underwater like an
immortal sprite, suspended outside events, but he'd then
imagined the running water would overflow and damage the
house, which would hurt Mom and possibly ruin Nat's insect
collection, and he'd hastily resurfaced to turn off the faucet in
time.

He then thought of the world as an enormous kid's collection of interesting stuff, some sweet, some grotesque. And,

there were funny things yet to see. Lying in the snow like an idiot was in itself funny. Even unfunny suicide is a reminder of how interesting life's plot is. Besides, Nat and Bonny and Minus had all offered him refuge, and the staff of Excelsior were poised to rescue him like a coed cavalry. Nothing was actually wrong. What's the problem? He wanted to bicycle.

Also, he wanted to watch Minus and Ruth's child grow up. He wondered what Hunter and Little Nat would be like as teenagers. Now he remembered the seventh party invitation, the one he hadn't been able to remember that morning, the invitation he had repressed in his mind. Little Justin from Excelsior was having an afternoon party and had invited Tad to it a week ago, the only adult he'd thought to include. The party was now long over, and he had done the right thing to miss it—he would have been arrested if he'd gone—but Justin had believed in him, at least as a worthwhile addition to his select guest list. Was the glass half-empty? Was the glass half-full? Even if the glass was empty, it was a perfectly fine glass, and it was unbroken. It could be refilled.

Tad called the Lord's name, as a Geronimo-like galvaniz-ing battle cry, and also, to his surprise, as a verbal thank-you note for the rescue. His body was his car, he then reasoned. He didn't need a lift from the Lord, he could drive himself. The chariots don't need to swing low, nor do the UFOS. Like adrenalized mothers who reflexively lift autos to save their child, he struggled to his feet in just a few seconds. *Allez-oop!* as if he'd just performed an acrobatic feat at an extremely untal-ented circus. Tad noticed the imprint his body had made in the snow, and it summoned up a childhood winter when he'd lain in the snow to make an angel. When he showed it to Nat, Nat had said, "Some wino must've passed out here!"

Tad oriented himself and emerged from the park on West Eighty-fifth Street, feeling a heady version of sober—after all, he'd napped and taken a polar swim simultaneously. He felt the sweet rush of landfall, from barrens to civilization, and the familiar storefronts and traffic lights of the West Side welcomed and reacclimated him to deceptively uninviting reality. He was dazed and still jacketless, but his regained safety displaced any feelings of cold. With no particular awareness of them, he sleepwalked awake past block after block of stolid silent mountains rife with concealed life, termite mounds wired for electricity, beehives, coral reefs, molds.

He found himself outside his building on Edgar Allan Poe Street. In his altered consciousness, he noticed as if for the first time the bodyless young face over the door, a stone decoration from the more gracious and unfair era when the town house had been built. Its features were eroded almost to illegibility—it could be a cherub or a satyr, or an old man's face, softened by time, for once—but that gave it a look of experience and complaisance. It wasn't Marley's frightening face in the door knocker, but an impartial observer's gentle remonstrance to Tad for his own superfluous agonized absurdity. Like a divine therapist, its silence was its advice. But it wasn't divine—Tad conducted a brief seminar with himself—it was a man-made blessing. The very unmiraculousness of this product was its power—not a vision, but a product of labor, grimy, pointless, a counterfeit of an imitation of a foreign fiction. Still, it gave pleasure. It floated in stone, impassive in decay, setting the stoic example the inanimate offers the animate.

Tad shivered, saw his breath, and remembered he was choosing to loiter in the freezing night.

"Tad Leary! What are you doing out with no jacket?"

It was his neighbor Estelle, returning home looking dreamy and downcast. If she had looked like a tired teenager that morning, she now looked like a child with progeria.

"Hi, Estelle! Uhh . . . just taking out some garbage!"

"But your shirt looks wet! Are you all right? You should get inside!"

Tad didn't want her to fret. "Well, you know the way you were playing hopscotch? I couldn't resist nipping into the park to make a snow angel!" It wasn't a lie, exactly.

"The snow's gorgeous, isn't it?" She dutifully looked toward Riverside Park, then into her purse to find her keys.

"How was Project Ex?"

"Well, all right . . ."

"You're getting home late." Tad reckoned it was after 1:00 a.m.

"Well . . . the braids worked." She found her keys. "I just don't think we're going to get back together or anything."

So, Tad thought. She had had seduction in mind.

A cab pulled up behind them as Estelle opened the building's front door. Roscoe emerged from the cab in street clothes, his suit carrier over his shoulder, and called, "Hey!"

"Roscoe!" Estelle called.

Roscoe bounded to their side. "Hey, man, you all right?" He noticed Tad was disheveled, wet, and jacketless.

"I am!" Tad replied, anxious to assure him. "I was, uh, playing in the snow!"

"Well, that's stupid! No jacket! I thought you got mugged!" Roscoe's voice suddenly turned from jovial holler to fury. "Hey!" The cab had driven off with his trumpet still in it. "Goddamn!" He dropped his suit carrier and chased the cab down the street.

"Oh no!" said Estelle. Tad debated whether he as a younger man should chase the cab, too, but it had already turned the corner and sped off.

Roscoe came back furious and despairing. "I knew something was wrong with that driver! He didn't even know how to *get* to West Eighty-fourth! I had to *direct* him!"

"You didn't get his name or cab number or anything, did you?" Estelle asked gingerly, looking for a possible solution without chastising him.

"No! Do you, when *you* ride in cabs?" Roscoe was entitled to be gruff. The three stood on the stoop for a silent minute, anticarolers.

"Is your name and address on it?" Tad asked.

"Yes," Roscoe fumed, as if saying no. Apparently, he didn't have much faith in "finders returners."

"Awww!" Estelle's voice tried to pour ointment. "I know the feeling! I left my grandmother's wedding dress in a cab! I was loaning it out for a play! I never got it back, but it didn't have my name or address on it."

Then the cab appeared from the opposite corner, having circled the block. Roscoe rushed to meet it. Its next customer had encountered the trumpet case, and the cabbie backtracked to return it.

"Hey! I appreciate it!" Roscoe shouted. He, in turn, handed the case to Tad, as if for momentary child care, and went back to the cab. He offered to augment his tip, which the cabbie cheerfully accepted. Roscoe called over his shoulder to Tad and Estelle, "It's Christmas, but it's still New York!" He then jokingly offered to tip the new passenger in the backseat, too, but Tad heard a man laugh and demur.

Without removing his trumpet, Roscoe lifted his trumpet case to his lips and pretended to blast a few notes of salvation. "*Ta ta da daah!*"

"Hallelujah!" said Estelle, which seemed a statement of "case closed" as much as anything, because she then exclaimed, "I am freezing to death! And Tad, you certainly must be!" She went inside, and the two men followed. She started up the stairs, calling back to Tad in the vestibule, "Get into a hot bath and dry clothes! Good night!"

As she disappeared, and Roscoe prepared to enter his apartment, Tad thought to ask him, "Oh, say—how was seeing your son?"

"Good! He's good, huge, healthy. He's in a band himself. It's Between Names."

"Oh, they don't have a name for it?"

"No, that *is* the name. You explain it to me!"

"And, how were your gigs?"

"No big deal."

Tad was impressed by Roscoe's failure to be impressed by Doozy's. He considered telling Roscoe they had just been at the same party, but he was confused and tired, and it might muddy the clarity of the shared trumpet rescue.

"I'm glad you got your trumpet back!" he said instead.

"You said it! I thought life was pretty evil for a minute there! Now I can feel like it's beautiful for a minute here!" He turned to open his apartment door. "Good night!"

"Yes, good night!" Tad climbed the stairs as fast as he could in his exhausted state. At last he was inside the apartment, like Superman in his contemplative Fortress of Solitude, safe from the surrounding arctic blasts. He stripped off his wet clothes and put on a white terry-cloth robe.

After sitting still for a minute, he was seized by an over-whelming urge to phone Angelo. He didn't want Angelo back. Their sexual relationship had never been at all tempestu-ous. It had only resembled a roller coaster in that the first great hitherto-unknown hill had been the most thrilling, and as time passed the subsequent hills got smaller and smaller, and the plunge more familiar, until the car began to race along a predictable straightaway, albeit still exhaustingly. Angelo had been his only long-term partner, but after five years, he'd gone from being Tad's fantasy amusement complex to being a pleas-ant public park. Tad knew trying to revive their relationship would be like trying to engineer the roller coaster to run back-ward, which gravity forbids. What Tad wanted was absolution from sin.

He phoned directory assistance in San Francisco and found Angelo was listed. Angelo was too modest and accessible a per-son to be unlisted. It was only about ten o'clock there, Tad cal-culated, and he dialed the number with the idea of revealing his epiphany, that Angelo had been his source of strength.

"Yes? Hello?" Angelo always answered the phone with a provisional readinesss to do the caller's bidding.

"Angelo? It's Tad," he said nervously.

"Tad! I knew it was you!" Angelo's voice was bright and excited. "I have a sick sense about these things! You know, like extrasensible perception!"

Tad was tempted to correct Angelo's vocabulary, which he'd always done when they lived together, but he now saw how complacent he had been, and besides, he was calling to apologize. "Am I calling too late?"

"Well, in all honestly, I was asleep. I work a breakfast shift tomorrow. But no big deal! You know how easy I fall asleep! Sixty to zero in ten seconds!"

Angelo had been the patient parent and he the child, not the reverse, as Tad had always imagined it. It was Angelo who had weathered Tad's sulks and tantrums, even if it was Tad who had always insisted on driving the car.

"It's your clear conscience, I guess," Tad answered.

"Aww, that is sweet." Apparently, Angelo wasn't going to punish him with silences.

"You won't believe this, but I ran into Donna and Jo Jo tonight!"

"Oh wow! That's right, they're visiting his sister! I'll see them next week!"

"She told me where you were, and I really wanted to give you a call!"

"Oh, great!" A touch of confusion sounded under Angelo's friendliness.

"So, how's life out there?"

"I like it, it's a whole new world for me. I got a little place on States Street, in the Castro. It's nice. A kitchenette, even a little balcony. All the anomalies of home."

"Great!" Now Tad began to wonder what exactly he intended to say.

"I miss my family, but for the time being, it's better here.

This'll be like my version of going to college. People are more into enjoying life here, there's less of that gut-wrinkling ambition like I'd see in New York. Plus, I don't feel *stupider* than everyone else out here!" Angelo had resisted moving from Waterville to New York, but he'd done it to oblige Tad.

"Are you doing any gardening?"

"Ha! I have potted plants on my balcony! Naw, I don't have any connections yet. Otherwise, I'm working at this place called Boo Boo Jaywalker's, down by Fisherman's Wharf. It's an eating and drinking *establishment*. That's what they call it, anyways."

"Oh, that's great. . . ." Tad just didn't know how to segue into apologizing.

Angelo sensed the significant stall. "Listen, I don't want to be posthumous here," he said carefully, "but if you're calling about getting back together again . . . I don't think it's a good idea."

Tad assumed he meant *presumptuous,* but with Angelo, you never knew. "No, no! I know that! I just wanted to wish you happy holidays and say how sorry I am that . . . I mean, if I hurt you." Now he felt like Dean.

"Aw, Tad! Our breakup was *supposed* to happen! I never would have guessed it was an excellent thing, but I know a whole new way of feeling now. Six months ago, even, I might have found it weird if you called, but you timed it good!"

"Um, are you in a new relationship?"

"No, that's exactly it! I lived with my parents until I moved in with you! I lived to please them and then I lived to please you! I lived for approval, and it is such a relief to live day to day without your identity having conditions. I like independence! I'm taking voice lessons!"

"Gee . . . So, that does sound like college."

"Yeah! An' I'm workin' in the dinin' hall, just like your gran'ma!" Angelo could intensify his townie persona when he wanted to. Like his gayness, he embraced it like a boy would a birthday puppy, whereas Tad, so far, had held both at arm's length.

They chatted for a few more minutes, which Tad intuitively sensed was better bridge building than Sternlandian serious talk would be. To his relief, this was the happiest possible unhappy ending.

"Tad," Angelo said at last, taking the initiative, "I gotta get some shut-eye or I'll be dropping omelettes in people's laps!"

"Can I call you again sometime?"

"Well . . . I'll leave that to your own discrepancy."

"All right. I will call—early in the New Year!"

"Okay, but don't approach it like you were creeping into confession! You're *absolved*!" Angelo knew his Tad all right. "Next time, call to trade jokes with me!"

"It's a deal!"

"Bye! And say hi to your family for me!" That was Angelo—a palace concealed under aluminum siding.

So, with forgiveness came another verse in his day's lesson on egotism. Angelo was a fuller person without him. Tad felt comforted and, despite the season, annoyed. Still, he resolved to work on that.

After hanging up the phone, Tad noticed the red blinking light on Garth's phone machine. There were three messages.

"*Tad, it's Minus,*" began the first, "*reminding you we're having dinner tonight. It's not that I think you'll forget, I just know actuality is not your long suit. Also, we may have a surprise for you! See you later!*"

"*Hey, it's Nat,*" went the second. "*Listen, since you're on hiatus now, I assume you're available to join us if we go to the Museum of Natural History tomorrow? See the Visible Dinosaurs? Sneer at them for being losers, while we're still respiring? Darth Vader here orders you to attend. Call me—we're staying at the Tantamount.*"

Lastly, there was a message from Gabe, with garbled party noise in the background. "*I hope Yoni gave me the right number. Tad? Look, you may not remember, but you gave me your wallet and ran out of the party. I hope and assume you got home safe, but come on, I know you need this. I get the 'vital organ' analogy now. Anyhow, I have to get back to bartending here, but call me and we'll figure out how to get this back to you."*

Tad poured a tall glass of water, the antidote to the antidote, hoping to minimize the next morning's interest-due payment on alcohol's levity loan. He reflected on his mixed lot, and saw that, on the genocide scale, he was doing all right. He might have a job, or not, and a place to live, or not, depending on his willingness to accommodate. He also might—though he knew it would take his best self's efforts—make a better fourth impression on Gabe. He thought of his mother's morbid optimism—"You could have been killed!"—and it buoyed him up, if only as a comforting reminder of her concern. Bear in mind, there may be Cheer, but there's no Getting Well.

He urged himself to go see his family on Christmas, and he hoped he would listen to that urging. For now, though, he fell into a deep sleep, from which even true love's kiss would not wake him, not that it tried.

In the dream that followed, he and Les and Nat were little boys again, and they were sailing on the open deck of a picturesque old tugboat like Popeye's, toward a hallucinogenic but perfectly natural sky of northern lights. Twelve-year-old Les stood at the bow, a figurehead of dormant Junior Achievement, with the wind in his longish hair. Nat fiddled with a slide rule, a device Tad hadn't seen in years. Why are we little boys again? Tad asked Nat Sci without speaking. It's the fact that we're headed toward the North Pole, smooth-faced Nat explained, also without words. It has to do with the magnetic poles. This is temporary, this will last only a few hours. When we head back toward the equator, we'll start to revert to our real ages. I'll get pubic hair, go through school, and meet Rekha, you'll take advantage of Angelo, Dad will die, then Mom. And, eventually, Les, then you, and I outlive you, interestingly. This is Indian Summer, our brains are delighted by facts rather than afraid of them, and our hearts are unaware of their own existence. Tomorrow is something good, very good, but it will be good for only several days. Since the big bang, the whole universe is just a fire that's slowly going out. But fires are beautiful to watch.

When Tad woke up the next morning, he was more dead than alive, but he got through the day, arranged to retrieve his missing vital organ, teased the dinosaurs with his loved ones, slept again, and the morning after that, on Christmas Eve Eve Eve, he woke up more alive than dead.

ALSO BY MARK O'DONNELL

"Wise and forgiving
. . . tough-minded and tender-hearted."
—*The New York Times*

GETTING OVER HOMER

This delicious "coming of middle age" novel takes a lyrical, winsome, and genuinely side-splitting look at heartbreak, aging, the search for home, and the madness of love between two mismatched men. The afflicted individual is Blue Monahan—twelfth of a swarming Cleveland brood—who came to New York City to seek fame and fortune and, of course, True Love—or, anyway, a safe haven and warm arms.

Fiction/0-679-78122-6